ONE LAST CHANCE

PAUL J. TEAGUE

ALSO BY PAUL J. TEAGUE

Morecambe Bay Trilogy 1

Book 1 - Left For Dead

Book 2 - Circle of Lies

Book 3 - Truth Be Told

Morecambe Bay Trilogy 2

Book 4 - Trust Me Once

Book 5 - Fall From Grace

Book 6 - Bound By Blood

Morecambe Bay Trilogy 3

Book 7 - First To Die

Book 8 - Nothing To Lose

Book 9 - Last To Tell

Note: The Morecambe Bay trilogies are best read in the order shown above.

Don't Tell Meg Trilogy

Features DCI Kate Summers and Steven Terry.

Book 1 - Don't Tell Meg

Book 2 - The Murder Place

Book 3 - The Forgotten Children

Standalone Thrillers

Dead of Night

No More Secrets

So Many Lies

Two Years After

Friends Who Lie

Now You See Her

PART 1

It took three swipes of the axe to hack off his finger. At last they realised this was no joke. They'd seen Sebastian's advertising antics on TV and knew that he was capable of pulling the most elaborate of stunts. Right up to the moment the axe had struck and they'd heard the sickening crunch of bone and sinew, they'd been convinced that the look of deadly seriousness on Sebastian's face would melt into a huge smile, the menacing group of men who'd burst into the room would begin to laugh, and it would all be over.

Jerry fell to the ground. He'd passed out from the shock. His livelihood would be ruined. They must have known who he was to target him so mercilessly. The leader of the gang, Baptiste, watched impassively as he slumped to the floor, his blood spilling crimson onto the cream carpet. He pulled the Rolex off Jerry's wrist.

'Half a million dollars,' he said, his accent betraying a hint of French. He held up the watch to the light ignoring the blood that was spattered along the wristband. 'I'd say that was worth losing a finger for, wouldn't you? Now, your jewellery please. I don't want to have to do any more damage to this lovely carpet. Mr Helix will be claiming on his accidental damage policy as it is. Let's not do anything hasty to further erode his enormous fortune.'

Without making a sound, the guests quickly followed his orders placing their jewellery in plastic bags. Watching from the safety of the doorway, Matt reckoned there must be a million pounds worth in one bag alone. He and Clare were out of their depth. They'd never fit in with these people. And now look at the danger he'd placed her in. He watched as one of the men – a skinny, unkempt lout called Leon, who looked like he needed a good bath – moved right up close to her, sweeping her long hair back across her shoulders, checking for anything which might be worth taking.

'Nothing on this one,' he shouted over to his boss. 'Just a wedding ring.'

Baptiste walked over, placing his hands on Clare's hips and running them slowly and threateningly up her waist.

'Interesting. Here is our cuckoo in the nest.'

'You leave her alone!' Sebastian shouted. Before he had time to speak again, a third man with a livid scar across his face had smashed his fist into the millionaire's chest, shutting him down instantly and leaving him writhing on the floor. Baptiste glared at the scarred man angrily, but said nothing.

Matt could see the guests flinching as they watched their host lying helpless and in pain. Their money counted for nothing here. It gave them no clout and no privilege. They were at the mercy of a bunch of pirates, at sea, in a place where nobody would be able to come and save them.

'Which one is your husband?' asked the man with the scarred face.

'Which of these snivelling little shits are you married

to? I'm guessing it's his money that gets you horny, not his stunning good looks ... not looking at the state of this lot anyway. What you need is a real man, someone who knows what a woman wants.'

He was right up close to her now. Matt held himself back with every last force of will that he could muster. He would kill that man. He would kill his grinning companions. And then he would return home with his wife, they'd continue living their crappy little lives, and he'd play no part in whatever it was that Sebastian Helix had got planned for him.

'Which one is your husband?' the man barked at her once again. Clare was crying now. There was no answer she could give to save Matt. Whatever she said, they'd be bound to find him. They knew how many people were in that place and there was no getting off, not until the storm died down. It would only be a matter of time before they located him.

Matt took a last look at his wife from the safety of the entrance to the bar area. Across the room he could see a man brandishing a machine gun, threatening the cowering chef and catering team, who were on their knees lined up against the far wall. Carefully, he let the swing door shut behind him, moved to the end of the bar and then headed off along the gently curved corridor.

They would come for him, of course. It didn't take a genius to work out that there was an extra table setting. They'd already figured out that Clare didn't belong. He knew that they were dispensable. They had nothing to offer: no bank account filled to the brim, no jewellery to sell on the black market.

Matt paused by the tray of drinks which had been left half-finished on the bar. He picked up the knife that the barman had been using to chop a lemon for a G&T, before he'd been bludgeoned and left to die on the floor. It was all he had for protection.

Behind him he heard a cry. It was Clare. The bastards. Frustration and helplessness seared through his body. He loved his wife more than anything. All he cared about was their life together. The deal with Sebastian Helix was meaningless in comparison. First he had to save his wife and then he was going to tell Helix and that bloody assistant of his where they could stick their investment money.

CHAPTER ONE

October, Helix Fort

'Look at the size of the place, Clare. It's incredible!'

'Does Sebastian Helix own all of it?'

'Apparently so. How much cash must you have to be able to buy something like this as your weekend retreat!'

'Amazing, isn't it?' Tucker's American drawl came over the headset. 'I've flown here more than a hundred times now and it never fails to take my breath away.'

He brought the chopper down on the helipad. The waves crashed beneath them, the sea was angry and grey.

'Here we are, welcome to Helix Fort.'

The blades slowed to a halt and Matt and Clare removed their headsets.

'I've never flown in a helicopter before,' said Matt. 'I hope the others didn't mind us skipping the boat?'

'It's no problem,' Tucker replied, shutting down the engine. 'Mr Helix invites a range of guests to the fort. You're not the first to have been given the chance to come by helicopter and you won't be the last!'

Matt looked at his wife. She was ashen.

'Are you alright, Clare?'

She nodded, even though she'd barely managed to hang onto the contents of her stomach.

'Just give me a moment, and I'll be okay. You know I'm a bad traveller.'

Matt felt a pang of guilt. He'd thought she'd enjoy the experience once they were up there. It was a once-in-a-lifetime opportunity. Clare needed a bit of a push from time-to-time, but maybe he'd been too insistent on this occasion.

Tucker gave her a couple of minutes to settle before opening the door. He was picking up Sebastian Helix next and didn't want to have to clean up vomit in the cockpit before his boss arrived. If they were held up it could mean missing the narrow window they'd got on the weather. Helix was over at Silicon Valley after this weekend and he'd be pissed if there were any delays.

'I'm okay now. Let's go.'

'There's Eddy. He's waiting for you. Some of the other guests have arrived already. You're safe to get off now, just prepare yourself for the wind when you step out. You don't get any windbreaks a mile out at sea.'

Tucker opened his door and stepped round to let Clare out.

'Blimey!' she grimaced as she stepped out onto the platform. 'You weren't joking when you said it would be windy.'

There was a chill to the wind. Autumn had arrived. Couldn't Helix have met them on that paradise island he owned instead of this place?

Between them, Matt and Tucker unfastened the suitcases and placed them on the helipad.

'Wow, you don't pack light!' joked Tucker.

'Well, you never know what you're going to need for a weekend with some of the world's richest people!' Clare snapped.

'I'm sorry,' Matt intervened, heading off a potential storm. 'We're both a bit tense. We live in a semi in Newcastle. We're not used to this.'

This seemed to calm Clare. He took Tucker to one side. 'She must have brought ten dresses. She's terrified she won't fit in. I told her to just be herself.'

'No need to explain. Helix is okay. Some of his guests can be a pain, but however much money they have, they all need to take a shit in the morning.'

Matt laughed at that. He wandered over to the solid painted line that marked the outer edge of the circular helipad and cautiously looked over the edge. There was netting to catch you if you fell, but the sea was wild, it would be a terrifying experience.

'Not too close!' Tucker called out as he lifted the two suitcases and walked towards Eddy who was waiting patiently.

'Matt, be careful!' Clare shouted as her husband recovered his footing after a sudden gust of wind. She was now happily chatting to Eddy, her long hair blowing around her face. She cursed that her hairband had snapped as she'd been playing with it before their helicopter journey. She hoped she'd have time to tidy herself up before she met any of the other guests.

As he turned around and headed over to his wife, Matt had no idea that he'd be forced to leap from that same helipad before the weekend was over.

CHAPTER TWO

October, Helix Fort

'We couldn't have asked for a nicer room. It's incredible what he's done to this place.'

'Yes, it was an eighteenth-century sea fort. I was lucky enough to accompany Mr Helix when he first came to look at it. It was very different then. He's spent a fortune on it. It works very well for him when he's back in the UK: he can come and go from here without the press on his tail all the time.'

'I've never had his and hers showers before. And that wardrobe is as big as our box room at home.'

Matt was walking around the room, examining everything.

'I take it we can connect our tech out here? I can't believe Sebastian Helix wouldn't have a decent internet connection in a place like this.'

Eddy smiled. It never ceased to amaze him that they

could be surrounded by all that wonder and all they were bothered about was getting connected to Netflix.

'Of course, Mr Dalton. Everything you need can be found in the leather folder on the desk. It's a superfast satellite connection and you'll have no speed issues, so long as it doesn't get too grey and stormy out there. You might struggle with your phone though, signals can be patchy.'

'What time will Sebastian – Mr Helix – arrive?'

Matt knew that it wasn't Sebastian Helix who was Clare's primary concern.

Mr Helix and Ms Winterton will be here by seven o'clock at the latest,' Eddy replied. 'I think you know Ms Winterton already, Mr Dalton?'

Matt's face reddened. He could feel Clare's immediate hostility.

'Yes, Ms Winterton and I have ... er ... we've met already.'

There was no hint in Eddy's voice to give away whether he knew or not, but he must have observed Clare's reaction. She looked as though she was about to throw something at Matt. Matt was beginning to wonder if it had been a clever idea to bring her with him after all.

'I'll leave you alone now, unless there's anything else I can help you with?'

They thanked him and he left them, shutting the door behind him. Neither Clare nor Matt could work out what Eddy Simmonds' role was. He seemed to be part-butler, part-host.

Left alone, there was a tense silence as Matt and Clare carefully considered their next words.

'Look, this weekend is business only, I've told you that—'

'You told me she wouldn't be here!'

They spoke at the same time, the mistiming of a marriage under strain. They'd lost their rhythm. Clare wasn't entirely sure that she wanted it back.

'The programme for the weekend doesn't mention her being here,' Matt replied contritely.

'Well, surprise, surprise. Here she is!'

'I told you, it was nothing, it was a mistake. What more can I do?'

'Not to have done it in the first place. How's that for starters?'

Clare's anger was always just below the surface. They'd agreed not to do the counselling thing, but maybe it had been the wrong decision. They needed to hang on a little longer – if Sebastian Helix went ahead with the deal, their troubles would be over. They'd be able to hire the best marriage counsellor in the country. They'd be able to bring in Deidre Sanders from The Sun newspaper for a personal consultation. They might even get their own photo case-book thrown in as a bonus.

'Just keep away from her. And don't let her anywhere near me!'

'I won't. I'll have to acknowledge her professionally, but anything more than that ... It's over. I love you. This is all about you and me.'

'I would have you rich or poor, Matt. You don't have to pull off this deal to impress me. I would have loved you – I do love you – as you are.'

Matt sometimes resented that his wife wasn't as driven as he was. Until he'd lost his job and it had been sink or swim, he'd never known that about her. When they were doing normal jobs, caught up in the regularity of a work routine, he'd never seen that in Clare. But she was unambitious. She didn't aspire to anything particularly challenging.

It had taken Sebastian Helix's Global Entrepreneur Challenge to make him realise that.

Clare's attitude was to cut their losses, move to a smaller house and sell the car to make ends meet. They'd lost well over half their income when Matt was made redundant, and they were hanging on by a thread. She never seemed to get that.

Besides, Matt had his pride at stake. He'd given himself two years to turn things around. He'd proclaimed to all his old workmates that he was an entrepreneur now, and there was no way he was ever going back to the nine to five. So, he'd set himself up for a nice fall. He was going to take this opportunity right to the edge.

That was the only reason things had gone too far with Victoria Winterton. She'd been around entrepreneurs a lot, and she knew what made them tick. When he'd met Victoria for the first time, they'd hit it off and the chat was easy. She'd reassured him about his ideas, and he felt that he fitted in, that his aspirations weren't crazy. That's why they'd got on so well that night. It's why they ended up in the bar together.

CHAPTER THREE

October, Helix Fort

There was a knock at the door. Had Eddy forgotten to tell them something?

'Come in!' said Matt, grateful for a distraction from the tension.

The gold handle turned and the door opened. A middle-aged couple were standing there, smiling. He was impeccably groomed, his black hair, greying at the temples and she was manicured to within an inch of her life. Money. Lots of it. Both Matt and Clare noticed it immediately.

They were dressed casually in jeans and T-shirts, but it was the trivial things that gave it away. Her earrings were pink diamonds and she wore a diamond-encrusted bracelet on her wrist. His watch oozed wealth. These were no bargain basement items from the Argos catalogue.

Clare's hair was still a mess and she was completely aware of how she looked. She ran her fingers through it as she rushed towards the door to greet their new acquaintances. Matt thought he recognised the couple, but couldn't place them.

'Hello, Phyllis and Vinden Jackson,' the woman began.

'Hello!' Matt walked over to join Clare, his hand outstretched to greet them.

'Matt and Clare Dalton, pleased to meet you!' Clare said, beating him to it. Here she was meeting her first millionaires and she looked like Ken Dodd on a bad hair day. Matt would have found it funny if he hadn't known how important it was to her to make a good impression.

He gave his best firm handshake. Would they know he wasn't one of them? They could probably smell it on him.

'So why has Sebastian invited you over for this weekend? I don't think we've seen either of you before,' said Vinden.

'Oh, we're imposters really. I've created a tech process that Mr Helix is interested in. He invited me over to discuss it this weekend—'

'He's being modest,' Clare interrupted. However angry she was with Matt, she was still incredibly proud of what he'd achieved. What he'd come up with could revolutionise the UK's internet access. Sebastian Helix had seen the opportunity and was keen to grasp it.

'Oh, I know. You're Seb's winner for this year, aren't you? I read all about it online. You're the Citywide WebHub guy. I'd love to hear about your big idea.'

Vinden seemed genuinely interested. Matt opted for the Reader's Digest version. He'd be making his pitch several times that weekend – he had no doubt about that.

'The basic idea is free municipal broadband access for every city and town in the UK. Using my system, we can create a dynamic infrastructure of high-speed broadband. Essentially, mobile phone owners and household broadband services make their unused data quotas available to free users and they get paid a credit for making it available rather than wasting it. It's subsidised by ad revenues. No more patchy broadband. No more having to register to access it.'

Clare could see that tech was not Phyllis's thing. It was the glazed look in her eyes that gave it away. Tech could be like football, religion or politics to a conversation: either it infused life and energy or killed it stone dead.

'So why are you here, then?' she blurted out, anxious to prevent Matt from explaining his idea further. She'd heard it a million times already. She'd been living with his concept since it was a seedling.

'We built this place!'

Phyllis smiled, clearly full of pride at their achievement.

'What, this entire fort ... or whatever it is?'

'We managed the renovation for Seb. Three million pounds it cost him. Bet he's regretting it now—'

'Philly, shh,' Vinden cautioned.

'They must have heard already.'

'Okay, but Seb's our friend. There's no need to stick the knife in.'

'Of course not, but if Matt here is seeking Seb's investment, it's only fair that he knows.'

There was no further protest from Vinden, so she continued.

'Seb's experiencing financial difficulties. You must have heard about that. That's why we're here – it's probably why you're here too.'

This was news to Matt and Clare. He was still receiving a start-up allowance from the government as an alternative to claiming benefits and Clare was working every shift that she could get at the restaurant. You tended not to hear the latest millionaire gossip in those lines of work.

'What's gone wrong?' asked Matt, sensing that a large fly might be about to land in the middle of his ointment.

'Seb's hanging on for dear life after that last thing of his went belly up. What was it ...? – a new cryptocurrency network. What was he thinking? It's the most volatile investment vehicle that's out there at the moment. Nobody even understands it yet. He was way too early to market.'

Phyllis shook her head in despair, and then carried on.

'We're here to buy this place back from Seb ... at a considerably lower price than he bought it from us. He'll need the money after the divorce. You know about that, of course. It's been in the papers.'

'Philly!' Vinden warned.

'You're here, no doubt, to resurrect his fortunes in the tech world. He needs a big win or he's going to be in the shit. I bet he's hoping that you're it!'

Matt looked at Clare. Like everyone else, they'd assumed that Sebastian Helix was unassailable in his wealth. After all, when you're living on considerably less than a thousand pounds a month, the kind of numbers that were mooted whenever Helix was on TV were unimaginable.

They stared into each other's eyes. Could they survive another disappointment? Maybe this would be the straw that finally broke the camel's back.

CHAPTER FOUR

September, Newcastle, UK

'I'm in the final selection!' Matt called down from the spare room. 'I've made it to the last ten projects.'

He ran down the stairs, trying to find Clare. He'd heard her moving around as she got ready for work. He always fancied her in her waitressing gear. It was the black that did it. And he loved it when she put her hair up, she always looked so hot when she went out to Franco's.

'You're looking great! Did you hear what I said?'

'Keep your hands off. I told you: no sex before work. I'll swear Franco noticed my stubble rash last time we risked it. I need this job now, more than ever. So keep it in your pants. And no, I didn't hear you shouting it from the rooftops, why would I?'

She gave him that sexy smile. She'd be too tired for any action between the sheets by the time she got home. He resolved to find something interesting online while she was out to relieve the tension. It would only take five minutes once he'd found a suitable video.

'What do you think? The last ten! At least I'm guaranteed a meeting with one of his advisers. That's better than nothing.'

'Yes, but it means you're going to be away for Isabelle's wedding. I'll have to go on my own now.'

'Come on, Clare. We discussed this. It's too important. You know I want to go to the wedding with you, but this could be my big chance.'

Clare checked her lipstick in the mirror and turned to him.

'I know, I know. Who's going to tell Isabelle though? You know she'll be disappointed.'

'She'll understand. She knows what her brother-in-law is like, and if I win ... well, life's going to change for all of us.'

'Did you think about what I said about the house? It's no sale no fee. We don't risk anything putting it on the market, and we might just need it.'

'Not yet. I'm certain we can hang on in there a little longer. Let's give it until after the selection weekend. If I get knocked out at that stage, I promise we'll put the house up for sale and I'll look for another job.'

Clare seemed uncertain, but she didn't want to discourage him. She was squeezing Franco for as many shifts as she could get, but he was beginning to moan about the downturn in the economy and how fewer people were going out at night. In fact, he'd been moaning for several months now.

'They're all Netflix and chilling,' he'd lament. He couldn't understand why everyone found this so funny.

Clare decided to give one more small push to try and change Matt's mind.

'You've seen the letter from the bank, haven't you?'

'The one on the mantelpiece?'

'Yes. Did you read it?'

'No, I don't need to. I know what they're saying: we can go three months into arrears then they'll call another meeting. I get my allowance paid on Friday. When you get paid, we'll reduce our arrears and pop a bit more on the credit card. It'll be fine. One more month, I promise.'

Clare gave him a kiss and walked towards the front door. It was getting harder to keep the faith. It's all very well having a unique vision of the future, but that doesn't pay the bills. She hated herself for being so unsupportive of Matt, but he was failing to grasp how serious things were. She didn't know if they would be able to recover if the house was taken from them, she couldn't even think about it.

Matt had been nurturing his idea for a couple of years, trying to figure out how to make it happen. It had become an obsession, which was taking them perilously close to the financial abyss. Sebastian Helix ran the Global Entrepreneur Challenge every year, and Matt had had his eye on it for quite some time.

'One day I'm going to win that competition!' he'd say to Clare. She'd reply that he sounded like Charlie Bucket in Willy Wonka and the Chocolate Factory. But she could see that he was deadly serious.

If pushed, Clare would have said Matt didn't have it in him. He lacked the stamina to see it through. But losing his job had changed it from a flight of fancy to a golden ticket. Entering it had been a long shot and he had done well to reach the final list of ten. It was a remarkable achievement.

As she headed out of the house for another evening of work, Clare resolved to list the property anyway. Matt would know the outcome of the selection weekend by the time it was all processed. The chances of him winning were low, even he knew that. He'd thank her for being so far-sighted, especially once the disappointment of losing had worn off.

Matt locked the door behind her and headed back up to the spare room. He'd read the letter from the bank – he knew what it said. He also understood that they were on a knife-edge, a house of cards ready to tumble at any moment. But his idea was good, everybody said so. If he could only get it in front of somebody like Sebastian Helix, he'd see the potential, he'd understand how lucrative it could be.

Matt sat at the desk and opened the link in the email. He'd have to book a train to London. They were paying expenses and he'd be able to travel first class. He hoped they paid up quickly because he'd spent up to their limit on the credit card. If they kept him waiting for repayment, the promise he'd made to Clare about paying down their arrears would be off the table.

Matt checked the email one last time then looked back at the notification attachment to see where to send it. It was a name that he'd be getting to know much better in the weeks to come: Victoria Winterton, Sebastian Helix's PA and general fixer, and the woman who would threaten his marriage and eventually their lives.

CHAPTER FIVE

October, Helix Fort

'I wonder if all of the other guests will be as interesting as Vinden and Phyllis,' Matt said as he walked to the bedroom window to look out over the sea.

'Do you think they were telling the truth about Sebastian? It seems a bit unlikely, doesn't it? The guy's rolling in it.'

'Do you remember that family across the road in the village when we were teenagers? The guy was working in Saudi. They were always broke – his wife used to come across the road to borrow eggs or flour. All fur coat and no knickers, isn't that what they say?'

Clare liked it when he referred to their teenage years. There was security in their shared history. It made her feel as if they could work through anything together.

'Shall we go and explore before he gets here? I reckon it'll be all business and best behaviour when he arrives.'

'Alright if I shower first? My hair's a mess, and I'd like to get it washed and dried. It might help my confidence if I tame it before I welcome the outside world.'

Matt nodded and looked out to sea again.

'It's grey as anything out there. I can barely see Portsmouth now. How exciting if we got trapped. They did warn us that coming and going depends on the weather.'

Clare was getting undressed by the bed and Matt's attention was diverted by this more interesting view. Normally he'd try his luck. She looked beautiful standing there. She always had been beautiful to him. Why had he been such an idiot?

He figured it was better if she made the first move. She was still very tense with him, and no wonder. What a fool he'd been to get caught like that. He watched her walk to the bathroom. She was making no attempt to cover herself up. Was it a come-on? He wouldn't risk it, he needed Clare onside this weekend. They were playing for the big prize.

She slipped off into the bathroom and Matt got his devices connected. There was no phone signal on the mobiles, but Eddy had warned him about that. He could hear the water running over Clare's body and every inch of him wanted to step in with her. It was a magnificent bath-room with massive showers, gold taps and luxurious towels and robes.

'How's the water?' he shouted through the door.

'Glorious!' came the reply, 'I haven't a clue how they manage it this far out to sea, but it's wonderful in here ...'

She paused. Matt thought the words *You should come in and join me* were on the tip of her tongue, but she stopped short. Once upon a time she'd have been eager to have him in there with her. He hoped he hadn't blown things forever.

As Eddy had promised, the internet connection was impressive. Like the water it ran freely and was much better than could reasonably be expected so far from the mainland. He checked his files, ran a test scenario and reassured himself that the tech would be fine. He was all set, ready to snatch that investment from Olaf bloody Strauss. Matt wondered when the smart-arse wunderkind would decide it was time to make his entrance. He'd been spared his presence so far, but it couldn't last long.

If ever you could have a nemesis, for Matt it was Olaf Strauss. He was blond, charming, perfectly toned and sported just the right amount of stubble on his chin. And he was amazing with his tech. For Matt, it had been a learned skill; he was not what the press like to call a digital native. Olaf Strauss was ten years younger. He'd dropped out of university completely confident that he knew better than any of the professors or academic staff. So far he'd been proven correct.

It seemed that the entire world was courting Olaf Strauss and his simple but inspired tech idea. He had figured out a way of keeping a smart-phone battery charged for over a week, with all the settings on full throttle and constant broadband use. He'd come up with some innovative technology; it was, as the corporates love to say, blue sky thinking – thinking completely out of the box. As millennials have a habit of doing, he'd approached the phone charge issue in a completely unique way. And now he was the most dangerous obstacle to Matt getting his own project funded.

For some reason, known only to his perfectly groomed self, Olaf wanted to work with Sebastian Helix. He could have worked with any one – or all – of the phone companies, but he was intent on winning Helix's mentorship. It had created quite a buzz around the competition. Matt wondered if Sebastian would be able to resist Olaf's proposition. His own idea was massive in its potential, but everybody who owned a smartphone wanted Olaf's concept straight away, even sooner if possible.

It was between the two of them. And while Clare was prickly about him being in the same room as Victoria Winterton, he knew that Olaf would be a distraction for her. He was one of those guys who was a magnet to women; he had an easy charm and made them laugh. The bastard. He was the kind of bloke all the women loved and the men despised, because, really, they wanted a touch of his magic.

'You okay? You look like you're brooding!'

Clare stepped out of the bathroom wrapped up in a gown while she towelled her hair dry. She looked a lot brighter.

'Just getting anxious about everything again.'

'Olaf Strauss?'

'What do you think? How about we push him into the sea while nobody's looking?'

Clare laughed. Sometimes, when they were chatting, everything was like it always had been.

She slipped off the robe and moved over to her suitcase, which was lying open on an oak stand. She looked perfect. Her body had barely changed since they'd become a couple, which was more than he could say for himself. He'd spent ten years working on computers for a living, and he knew he'd let himself go. If the money came in when his idea took off, he'd change that. He'd stop working so hard and pay more attention to the important things, like staying in decent shape for his wife.

'What should I wear?' she asked, working her way through her clothes.

'It looks like you've brought everything you own.'

'I've never mixed with millionaires before. I don't know how they dress. I thought I'd better come prepared for any occasion.'

'Jeans and a shirt are fine in most situations, and if we're going outside, tie your hair up, it's blowing up out there. But you're fine. Seriously, just be yourself. These people don't bite.'

Clare seemed uncertain, but followed Matt's guidance despite her doubts. Jeans and a shirt it was. She blow-dried her hair. She'd brought spare hairbands and slipped in a couple of hair clips in case. She'd learned her lesson making the short walk over from the helipad to the entrance.

Maybe it was because of her job, but Clare had a lovely, effortless way with people. She dealt with more than eighty people each night in the restaurant – you had to have a way with people to manage that. But always she was the small village girl at heart, doubtful of her right to be there, suspecting that she wouldn't fit in.

They stepped through the riveted iron door of their suite into the curved corridor. The use of ironwork in the structure was in stark contrast to the quality of the furnishings and fittings. Matt usually hated all that House Doctor stuff, but even he appreciated the subtle fusion of styles.

It was quiet. They couldn't hear anybody else about. They knew that some of the guests were travelling via a later boat, but weren't sure if they'd arrived yet.

Tucker had flown off to pick up Sebastian Helix from the local airport. There would be some staff members there and no doubt the usual entourage that followed a man like that.

'Shall we head up to the lighthouse?'

Clare had regained her spirit of adventure. It was like having a funfair all to yourself.

'Sure, why not?' Matt felt like a child, wanting to explore everything at once. It was an incredible structure. He wondered how a couple such as Vinden and Phyllis even knew where to begin managing a project like a fort renovation. Builders were unreliable at the best of times – what must they be like when their latest project was out at sea?

The lighthouse was spectacular. It gave a 360-degree view all around the fort. There was information on the walls explaining how the structures had been built in the 1800s to protect the south coast of England from the French. It seemed incredible to Matt and Clare that the forts were that old.

'You can see the Isle of Wight on a cloudless day, but no chance of that today!' Matt laughed. 'It looks a bit autumnal out there, I'm not sure if we'll be using those hot tubs this weekend. I think we'll all be huddled around that fire pit! Look at the size of it.'

'I hope we will,' Clare said, looking down at the collection of three tubs on the deck below them. 'They're screened well enough, and with the water warmed up they should be fine. I bought my swimming suit. I've never been in a hot tub before. I'm determined to give it a try, even if it's for only five minutes before I freeze to death!'

There was the sound of voices coming up the stairs. They were no longer alone. It was time to meet some of the other guests. They couldn't have been more surprised as the familiar faces emerged around the corner of the curving staircase. It was as if they'd walked onto the set of a TV show. Standing in front of them were three household names: Quentin and Hunter, the gay couple from TV's

Glorious Gardens, and Riff, the guitarist from the recently split rock band, Rancid Knights.

Matt felt Clare trying to disappear into the background. She was looking for a second exit, immediately panicked by the presence and celebrity of the new arrivals. Perhaps they were both way out of their depth after all.

CHAPTER SIX

October, Helix Fort

'Hey, you're Matt Dalton! Pleased to meet you.'

It was the last thing they'd expected. And he had such a cultured voice too, immediately putting them at their ease as he approached enthusiastically with hand outstretched.

'Hi, pleased to meet you … er … shall I call you Riff?'

Matt shook the guitarist's hand. He noticed the Rolex watch attached to his wrist. He'd never even seen a real one before. He wanted Clare to take a picture so he could post it on social media. There he was, Matt Dalton, shaking the very hand that had launched a thousand amazing electric guitar solos.

'Just call me Jerry. Riff is my stage name, I don't use it among friends. Jerry Daniels.'

He smiled at Clare and brought her into the conversation. He could see that she needed a lifeline.

Matt reminded himself that Riff also shook his dick with that hand. He was only human, he had to remember that. They mustn't make themselves look like idiots. This was a business event, and they needed to behave appropriately. He still wanted that selfie with Riff though.

Quentin and Hunter stepped forward and joined in the introductions. They seemed tense. Matt didn't watch much terrestrial TV, he was more a Netflix guy, but at one time it was impossible to miss Quentin and Hunter and their Glorious Gardens programme. It was an hour of summertime TV fun, with celebrities teaming up with ordinary gardeners to see who could create a garden fit for royalty. The winner got to makeover an area at Balmoral as their prize. Plus there would be the inevitable book deal, TV adverts and so on. It was like an X-Factor to discover a new Alan Titchmarsh. Definitely not Matt's thing, or Clare's either.

But he'd seen enough Facebook posts to know that the show had recently been cancelled. One of the contestants had said something homophobic and Quentin had struck him across his face with a cucumber. It had already become that year's YouTube sensation, but despite a huge public outpouring of support for the couple, Quentin's contract had been terminated. Quentin and Hunter were a double-act, like Ant and Dec, but unlike Ant and Dec they were also a couple. So, wherever Quentin went, Hunter followed. They were currently in between jobs.

They seemed friendly enough, but Matt picked up on the tension between them. He recognised it because he was living it out in his own relationship. It was a strained cordiality. Matt and Clare knew all about that. It had become their constant companion over the past fortnight.

For a moment, Matt was tempted to make a joke about Quentin having a cucumber hidden behind his back. He had to stifle a stupid grin and look away as he struggled to contain his giggling at the thought. Fortunately, Clare stepped forward and saved him.

'We're so pleased to meet you all, and how flattering that you've heard about Matt's work.'

'Seb told me all about it,' said Jerry. 'I always take an interest in this stuff, you know. There are so many challenges in music these days with iTunes and Spotify. When we hit the big time in the eighties all we had to worry about was the colour of our 12-inch singles: red, yellow or blue – that was it.'

Matt was grateful for the comment, it gave him an excuse to be smirking. He rejoined the conversation, while Quentin and Hunter went off to admire the view from the top of the lighthouse. Separately.

'I was gutted when you guys announced that you were finally splitting up. It feels like you've been around all my life.'

'Steady, I'm only 63,' Jerry said. 'Plenty of life in the old guitarist yet.'

'What brings you here for the weekend?' asked Clare.

'You must know about the court case. After all these years and my recent divorce from my now extremely wealthy twenty-five-year-old wife, I find myself on the verge of having to sell my last house. I'm hoping that Seb will back my solo career, work a bit of his magic and get things going for me again. I've got over thirty new tracks ready to roll.'

Matt was beginning to wonder if Sebastian Helix was assembling a collection of birds with broken wings in his private fort. Only Phyllis and Vinden seemed to be on a lucky streak so far and that was only because they were picking over the ashes of the Helix fortune.

'I'd like you to keep that to yourself,' Jerry added. 'Don't breathe a word to that journalist cow Kylie Parker. She's from CelebUK magazine and Seb's invited her for the weekend. She was the bitch who broke the news of our split. I'd got pissed and was mouthing off about my wife running off – with the drummer from Tense Macabre of all people. She overheard me. I was upset. She shouldn't have done that.'

Matt knew who Kylie Parker was. She was an attractive lady. This was becoming quite a party.

'Oh, Kylie Parker, I'm a huge fan,' said Clare, who'd perked up now the fear of celebrity was starting to wear off. 'I love her fiction. I don't read the magazine, but I couldn't put her last book down.'

'Steer her away from me please, especially if I've had a drink or two. I don't need any more headaches in my life.'

Quentin and Hunter seemed to have resolved whatever it was that had been bothering them and had come together over their shared love of gardens. They were speculating about how the deck of the fort could be brought alive with a selection of shrubs and flowers. Their ideas sounded both ambitious and expensive. Surely Helix couldn't be experiencing cash-flow problems?

Kylie Parker stepped up into the lighthouse's viewing area and the mood changed instantly.

'Kylie,' Jerry nodded. There was no love lost between those two. The atmosphere was positively hostile.

'Hi Jerry!' Kylie teased, striding up to him and touching his arm. She was being a bitch.

Clare lost her default shyness and intervened, engaging Kylie in discussion about how much she loved her work. She turned to introduce Matt, but he'd sloped off with Jerry to talk about music. He couldn't believe it, he was in the presence of one of his greatest musical idols, and they were hanging out and chatting like friends. This is what had got him into trouble with Victoria. It was that taste of another life, a new world, one which Matt desperately wanted to be a part of. And maybe … it was hard to say … maybe one in which Clare would not flourish.

He looked over in her direction. She was perfectly comfortable with Kylie, but any mention of business, seed funds, angel investment or share options, and she glazed over, almost to the extent that she was rude. If she was going to become his trophy wife in that environment, she'd need to step up.

Quentin and Hunter were suddenly shouting and pointing. A helicopter had emerged from the gloom and was hovering over the landing zone. Tucker was having diffi-culty landing, buffeted by strong gusts of wind, but before long he set the chopper down. He waited for the blades to slow before stepping out and opened the door facing towards the sea.

Two figures emerged, a man and a woman. Matt couldn't see who it was at first, but he hoped he might be spared Olaf's presence for another hour or two. There was a familiarity in the way the man walked. He had a purpose and confidence about him, it had to be Sebastian Helix. And at his side was a woman, immaculately made-up, tall, attractive and exuding self-confidence. They were clearly comfortable with each other.

Not for the first time in that viewing area, the atmosphere changed.

'Oh look, it's Seb!' squealed Quentin. 'He's early. At last we can get this party started!'

Clare sidled up to Matt and muttered tersely under her breath.

'And that, I assume, is his stupid whore of an assistant?'

CHAPTER SEVEN

September, Newcastle, UK

'We've got a big party coming in tonight, twenty of them at ten o'clock, I'm afraid.'

'Really, Franco? They'll be hanging about until at least midnight.'

'We need these customers, Clara. You know I can't be turning business away, things are just too tight.'

He always called her Clara. He claimed his family came from Naples, but she was convinced that he was as Italian as she was. She'd let it slide a long time ago.

That didn't stop Zoe mimicking him when he was back in the kitchen.

'We need these customers, Clara,' she said in a faux Italian accent, 'It's because our food is so shit that we have to be thankful for what we can get.'

Clare laughed and put her finger to her lips to encourage Zoe to lower her voice. They were setting up the tables. The first guests were due anytime soon. It was the calm before the storm.

'That lot from the rugby club are in tonight. You watch, I'll bet I can squeeze a twenty quid tip out of them.'

Zoe undid a button on her blouse, revealing a blue lacy bra underneath.

'Give them a good flash of your tits and they always tip well. I'm going for a full lean-over tonight. When I come out with the banana sundaes, you watch, they won't be able to keep their eyes off them.'

Clare laughed.

'What, the sundaes? You're terrible. Emmeline Pankhurst would say you're a traitor to your gender.'

'Hey, I still vote, but I get my tits out from time to time to beef up our shitty wages. You should try it, you know. You've got way better jugs than me. I'll bet you: you serve the rugby guys, and if you don't make twenty-five quid, I'll buy you a drink once we've finished our shift. What do you say?'

Clare was thinking about it. She could hardly believe it. Twenty-five pounds was three hours work, slightly more. It was only a flash, after all.

'You should let your hair down more often. You're a walking sex bomb and you don't even know it. That's what comes of sleeping with the same guy all your life. You don't know what you've got to offer. I hope he appreciates you.'

The problem for Clare was that Matt didn't seem to be appreciating her. He was so preoccupied with this Helix Corporation thing that he was living in another world.

'You should have slept around a bit before you married. I can't believe you've only ever slept with one guy in your life.'

She and Matt had been together forever. They'd

married at nineteen and missed out the usual university thing. Matt always had big dreams. It was endearing when he was eighteen, less so now he was thirty-two.

She did sometimes wonder if they should have split up, if even for a while – sow their wild oats and all that stuff. But when she heard about the escapades that her friends had with men – Zoe'd had chlamydia three times and seemed to be waxing any bit of hair below her neckline every week – she was thankful for Matt. The grass didn't appear to be any greener on the other side of the fence. Most guys seemed to be incapable of making a commitment; they were always onto the next thing. She didn't want that kind of life.

If it meant missing out on the occasional opportunity, it was fine by Clare. That was the small price she paid to be with a man like Matt. Still, with things as they were, she was going to accept Zoe's challenge. She knew she was in decent shape. Matt mentioned it often enough and her own mirror told her so.

She'd been against it when Matt had suggested getting new wardrobes with full-length mirrors but, truth be told, she liked to watch them having sex. It was like having your own porno without having to upload anything to the internet. And it turned her on, watching her own body writhe and tremble like that. Sometimes, and she would never admit this to anyone, especially not Zoe, she pretended it was someone else that she was straddling. There was no harm in it. All the magazines say it's healthy to fantasise from time-to-time. It was nobody in particular. Just some other guy. He was faceless.

'What do you think of this?' she said, undoing two of the buttons on her shirt. She leant over the table so that her cleavage was pointed directly at Zoe.

'You sexy cow, I can't possibly compete with that. There's a tiniest touch of nipple there too, you saucy minx. I'm telling you, if you do a lean-and-gleam tonight, you'll double your wages. Every table with a bloke who isn't blind or gay. I promise you.'

It was a long night. There was a lull just before the big party came in when Clare had a moment to message Matt and let him know that she'd be back after midnight.

NP, he'd replied. *I'm up working. I'll be here when you get back. I'll meet you – give me a ten-minute warning when you finish.*

Clare knew that Matt wouldn't relish the thought of being in the city centre at that time of night, but he'd like the idea of her walking home even less. And with the car now sold to make ends meet, it was walk or taxi.

Clare made over fifty pounds in tips that night. She felt naughty doing it, but Zoe was right, it worked a treat. The guys couldn't keep their eyes off her and they flirted openly, even if their wives were sitting there right in front of them. It was some macho man thing, slipping in a tenner as if it was some great gesture or favour they were doing her. It was the waitress equivalent of tucking a note in her knickers at a strip club.

She felt sexually empowered by the experience. She'd never done anything like it before. It was good to know that she could make other men hot for her. For a few hours she felt part of Generation Tinder.

'Told you!' Zoe gloated. 'Oh, and by the way, don't beat yourself up that my tips were down tonight. Those wonderful titties of yours have given me a right good run for my money. I'm going to have to go out begging tomorrow to make it up now.'

'Oh, I'm sorry,' Clare said. 'I really didn't think it would work as well. Don't mention it to Matt. I don't know how he'd feel about us topping up our income like that.'

'Is he still working on that app thing? How long is he going to give it? It's been going on for some time.'

Matt's dreams were becoming an embarrassment. Clare had a friend whose baby had been three weeks overdue. Everywhere they went, people would ask, 'Not arrived yet?' That's how she felt about Matt's tech project. Only this baby would be full-grown by the time it came out.

She sipped her lager and forced a smile for Zoe.

'Don't worry, Zoe. By this time next year, we'll all be millionaires.'

Franco had finished clearing up the kitchen and walked into the bar area. The staff were paid in cash from the till, but it was no concern of Clare's how he managed his accounts.

'Girls, I'm sorry, but I'm going to have to let you both go.'

It was the last thing they'd expected. Why hadn't the bastard told them before the shift started? Because he wanted to make sure they were smiling for that large group, that's why.

'You're kidding?' Clare said, panicking. She was working out the money. Even with that pay packet and the generous tips, they'd be short on the mortgage.

'I'm so sorry. I have to close the restaurant and work for my brother. I can't keep this going any longer. My lease is up, I have to walk away now.'

'You might have warned us, Franco, you tosser!'

Zoe was angry. She'd only paid for a holiday abroad the week before.

'It happened very fast. I thought I was going to be able to keep things going, but I can't. I daren't renew the lease.

I'm sorry, girls. If it's any consolation, let's drink the bar as dry as we can. Anything you want. On the house.'

Clare had forgotten to message Matt to come and pick her up. She texted him to let him know that she was staying late and she'd get a taxi home. She kept the job loss bit to herself.

It was like the wake of a very elderly person. Nobody was crying. It had been expected, in a roundabout way, but everybody had hoped the end wouldn't come. There was laughter tinged with great sadness, and when it was over they were left with that lingering sense of loss.

Clare didn't take a taxi, she wanted to walk home. It was past two o'clock by the time they'd had enough, and that was late enough to be clear of the pissed-out-of-their-brains brigade. The city centre was quiet; she felt safe.

She wanted to cry. How the hell were they going to dig themselves out of this hole? She hadn't got the courage to tell Matt. She'd keep it to herself and tell him that the restaurant was closed for refurbishment for a couple of weeks. She'd let him attend his conference, but then they'd have to get serious. The house would have to go – they would need to rent a one-bedroom flat or something like that. They'd make it work. They'd been in social housing as teenagers. She'd thought they were clear of all that when they'd finally bought their first property.

Clare crept into the house. Matt had left the hallway light on for her, he was considerate like that. She turned it off, removed her shoes and slowly made her way up the stairs. The light was still on in the spare room.

'Matt,' she whispered. 'Are you still awake?'

There was no reply.

She pushed open the bedroom door. Matt was asleep, his head resting on the keyboard, his glasses placed to the side. He'd crashed out waiting for her. She went to touch him gently on the arm, to rouse him so that he could come into the bedroom to sleep. She looked at what he'd been reading on the screen. It was a LinkedIn profile for the woman that Matt had mentioned, Sebastian Helix's PA, Victoria Winterton.

Clare hadn't realised until she saw that profile picture quite how attractive Victoria was.

CHAPTER EIGHT

October, Helix Fort

Matt knew that the weekend was bound to be difficult with Victoria there. He'd been a stupid idiot. For a while the power, the money – the sheer excitement of it all – had overcome him and made him lose sight of the end goal. He'd have kept it quiet. It was only a one-time thing and there was no need for Clare to know, but that plan had been scuppered by the photograph. He'd fallen right into the trap.

There was a buzz at the top of the lighthouse as they looked out of the huge windows to monitor Sebastian's arrival. He was an entrepreneur whose fame was on a par with the biggest celebrities. His presence could excite the rich and famous, turning them into fawning fans, his incredible wealth exceeding even theirs. Yet, if Phyllis and Vinden were to be believed, that was all a facade.

'The man oozes brilliance,' Riff commented. 'He's at the other end of the fort but you can feel his power from here.'

For Matt, that comment was surreal. Riff was a guitarist

who, in his day, had filled stadiums with thousands of screaming fans. One of his famous guitar solos would have the entire crowd at his command, chanting for him to give them more. Yet here he was as Jerry Daniels, a normal guy getting excited by a bloke coming out of a helicopter.

Matt was trying to follow Victoria's progress along the helipad, but he knew that he was being closely scrutinised by Clare. He wanted to figure out what had happened that night, whether she was really that attractive, and why he'd been so stupid as to fall for the oldest married-man trick in the book.

'He still looks good, even if Ruby has gone off with the kids now.'

Hunter was referring to Sebastian's acrimonious divorce. Another marital break-up. It made Matt even angrier with himself. He and Clare had a good thing going, he knew that. There were challenges – weren't there in any marriage? – but he wanted it to work. He didn't want to end up like Seb and Riff.

'What's the protocol here?' Clare asked Kylie. The pair had hit it off immediately. You'd have thought they were old friends already, the way Clare spoke.

'I'm here on Seb's payroll this weekend, rather than as a reporter. It's the done thing to leave Seb alone until he emerges from his suite in the early evening. No knocking at the door or anything like that. When he emerges for early evening drinks, that's it – he's one of us then. Only he's not one of us, of course. He's stinking rich and we all want to feed off him in some way.'

Sebastian, Victoria and Eddy disappeared into the main building below. Eddy was like an attentive butler, but his status was clearly much higher than that. He was no odd-job man, but nobody seemed to know what his relationship to Sebastian was. He was always there, continually making sure that things ran smoothly.

'I'm going exploring with Kylie, is that okay?' Clare asked, taking Matt by surprise. It was the last thing he'd expected. He'd thought that Clare would want him close by all weekend to bail her out if she felt out of her depth. Now though she was off with one of her favourite authors exploring a millionaire's private fort.

'Of course it's fine. Off you go. We'll meet back at the room at six o'clock if not before. You can't get too lost here. It's just a big circle. Enjoy! I'll see you later.'

He went to give her a kiss. She tensed at first, but then moved her cheek towards him. Maybe the distraction of this weekend would help to thaw things a little.

Matt watched as the women made their way down the stairs, chatting away, already at ease with each other. He looked around, wondering what his next move would be. He'd have to speak to Victoria soon, he'd need to handle that one carefully. If he was lucky, he'd run into her while Clare was off the scene, and they'd be able to get any awkwardness out of the way before they were seen in public.

He looked at Riff – or Jerry as he'd have to get used to calling him – searching for a clue as to what happened next. Hunter and Quentin were making their excuses, following Clare and Kylie down the stairs, heading off to their room for an afternoon nap.

'Looks like that leaves us, Matt. Fancy stepping out on deck?'

'Yes, why not? I take it you mean the garden area down there with the seats?'

'Yeah, it's sheltered – they've surrounded it with windbreaks – and you can get a drink at the bar. Might as well make the most of the daylight. It looks like we're in for some shitty weather.'

Matt agreed. The light was slowly beginning to fade and already floodlights were being switched on around the top deck. Jerry was right, there was plenty of shelter in the garden area and he was pleased to find that he could get a decent pint of beer from the bar. He hadn't been aware of any staff other than Eddy, but he reasoned they must be about the place. Someone had to change the sheets and clean the toilets.

'Do you reckon he's going to fund your idea?' Jerry asked.

'Who knows?' Matt replied, honestly. 'I think when push comes to shove, Olaf will win it. He exudes confidence and charm, and I don't have that. Besides, Olaf's concept could be bigger than mine and it will be faster to hit the market.'

'You've heard Seb is in trouble, haven't you?' The divorce is expected to knock him back and he's had a couple of misfires recently. I was talking to Gina and David earlier. They think he's got us here this weekend to line up his ducks in a row.'

'Gina and David?' Matt racked his brain, trying to figure out if he knew a Gina and David from TV or the papers.

'Gina and David Young. You've probably never heard of them, but they're gurus to the stars. Like a rich man's Tony Robbins. They made their money with some kind of multi-level marketing scheme – health and wellbeing it was, but you wouldn't know it from the size of their arses. Anyway, they're rich and they know how to turn some wealth into more wealth. That's why they're here. Watch their dogs, by the way. Little bastards they are. I don't know why Seb allows them onto the fort.'

'I've never heard of them. I assume they're American if it's multi-level sales?'

'No, British, but made their money in the States. Quite a quaint couple really. No kids, too much cash – that's why the dogs are so spoiled.'

'What's this weekend all about then? I know why I'm here, but I thought it would only be me and Olaf and a couple of Sebastian's celebrity friends. You reckon it's something more than that?'

'Definitely! Look who's here. Quentin and Hunter and me, we're what you call resting assets. All three of us are bidding for career revivals: potentially there's a lot of money to be made from all of us. Then Kylie Parker, she's hot property as a writer. I reckon he wants her to write a book about him. He's not done the official book of his life yet – have you noticed? That'll bring in some income. And Gina and David, they're here to advise on the money; they don't miss a trick those two.'

'How about Vinden and Phyllis? They reckoned they might be buying this place off him.'

Jerry raised his drink to his mouth and as his shirt cuffs pulled up, Matt noticed once again the stunning Rolex watch. Very nice it was too. He claimed to be broke, but being broke seemed to have a different definition for the rich. For Matt and Clare it would mean a repossessed home and a life on benefits. For these people it appeared to be more a case of losing a mansion and re-releasing your back catalogue.

'Don't believe everything you hear from those two. They're marginally worse than David and Gina's dogs, only a little less snappy. Oh, and they don't shit on the deck either.'

Matt laughed out loud at that, but he noticed a slur in Jerry's last sentence. He was halfway down his pint of beer, and Jerry was on the wine. Had he been drinking already?

From the corner of his eye, Matt caught sight of Clare and Kylie moving into the bar area. Clare hadn't spotted him out on the deck. He watched his wife as she and Kylie sat on the bar stools and ordered what looked from afar to be cocktails. They were laughing about something or other.

'Can you hear that?' Jerry asked.

Matt listened.

'It's the generators, isn't it? You can hear them from our room. I take it we're in the cheap seats? I'll bet Sebastian's room is well away from the engines.'

'No, not the generators. You block those out after a while. It's another engine noise – sounds like a boat.'

'Yes, now you mention it, I can. That must be why there's a lighthouse on top of this thing. We're quite close to the shore, there must be boats passing by all the time—'

There was a crash from the bar. It was a glass breaking as it fell to the floor. Jerry had distracted him from watching Clare as she chatted and laughed with Kylie.

'You bloody bitch!' came Clare's voice.

It looked like Victoria Winterton had just met his wife.

CHAPTER NINE

October, Helix Fort

Matt had never seen Clare behave like that. When they were younger, at secondary school, she'd been jealous of the other girls in their year, always suspecting them of plotting to get their hands on him. But once the social abomination that is secondary education was over, she grew sure of her position by his side. The incident with Victoria Winterton had really knocked her confidence.

'Why couldn't you have kept your hands off him, you stupid cow!'

Kylie was trying to keep Clare away from Victoria, who was looking bewildered. Matt's face reddened.

'I smell a catfight!' Jerry grinned at him. 'Who's been a naughty boy then? You'd better go and put that right. I think your wife is about to kill Seb's PA.'

Matt jumped up from his chair, half-hoping that the situation would have resolved itself by the time he got there. It had, kind of.

Victoria seemed stunned. She clearly wasn't used to being confronted by Seb's rich guests. Clare was crying and being comforted by Kylie. The barman was sweeping up the glass.

'Jesus, Clare. Please tell me you didn't throw a glass.'

'Give her a few minutes,' Kylie said quietly, indicating that he might do better to make himself scarce for a moment. 'I'll take her into the ladies to get herself tidied up.'

Once they'd gone, Matt nodded at Victoria.

'I see you've met Clare.'

'If it's any consolation, she didn't throw the glass, she knocked it over with her elbow when she turned around to scream at me. But yes, we've met. Thank you for asking.'

'You know she knows?'

'I'd figured that out. I take it it's not gone down too well at home?'

'You could say that.'

Matt considered her face, trying to work out what had attracted him to her. She was glamorous, yes, but in a made-up, well-groomed, highly manicured kind of way: not his regular type of woman. That was Clare. So what had sparked things off between them?

'How are you, Victoria?'

'I'm fine, Matt. A little shocked, but I'm fine. Are you excited about the weekend?'

'There's a lot riding on it. I hope this incident won't count against me with Sebastian. I'll talk to Clare and make sure it doesn't happen again.'

He was relieved that they were talking and she'd moved onto safer ground. There was no chance of a replay with this woman. He couldn't understand what had happened. He didn't fancy Victoria. There was no connection there. Had he been carried away by the moment?

'I promise not to tell him about it. He'll be out shortly – he's making a few calls. He's looking forward to seeing you ... and Olaf.'

'Speaking of whom, has he arrived yet? I've not seen him, or heard him yet.'

Victoria smiled at that. She was more attractive when she smiled. Her face was quite stern otherwise.

'No, no sign of Mr Strauss yet. I'm sure we'll all know when he gets here. He's the last to arrive ... wouldn't you know it. He'd have to be here after Sebastian so he can make his big entrance.'

This was more comfortable territory for him. He could remember them chatting about Olaf Strauss. Olaf had made an unwelcome pass at one of the female finalists in the competition and she'd slapped him across the face. It was straight out of a 1950s movie. Matt had chuckled to himself at the time. Who slaps men across the face these days? Most women he knew would have kneed him in the bollocks.

He and Victoria had a shared dislike of Olaf. It wasn't only that Olaf was his more handsome, charming, talented and wealthy opponent in the contest. Although, of course, it was partly that. He was just a dickhead. Regardless of the competition, in any other environment Matt would still have wanted to punch his lights out. And he was not a violent man.

'Any clues as to Sebastian's thinking?' he asked, fishing for a hint of how the weekend might play out.

'Come on, Matt, you know I can't tell you anything. But you've got a great idea. Sebastian loves it. You wouldn't be here if he didn't.'

Matt thought about asking her the question that had been on his lips since Clare had received the email. He'd asked her twice via LinkedIn, but she hadn't given an answer, brushing him off with an *I'm as confused about that as you are* line.

Clare and Kylie returned to the room. He thanked his lucky stars he and Victoria hadn't been in the middle of that conversation. Clare would have sensed it immediately.

'Clare, I'm sorry we got off to a bad start. I'm Victoria Winterton, Sebastian's PA.'

She held out her hand. Clare had been crying, and her eyes were still red. She considered shaking Victoria's hand for a moment, but thought better of it.

'You'll forgive me if we don't become best mates straight away, but I'm sorry about that outburst. It won't happen again.'

Victoria retracted her hand. The tension was becoming unbearable.

'Did I miss some drama?'

It was a new voice, confident, well-spoken, assured of its position in the world. Sebastian Helix had walked into the room.

'Hello, Matt. Good to see you again.'

Sebastian took Matt's hand and shook it enthusiastically, gripping his lower arm with his left hand. Matt wondered if he was being given a Freemason's handshake, being tested to see if he was part of some secret club.

'And this must be your lovely wife. I'm pleased to meet you, Clare.'

Matt clocked how Sebastian adeptly chose to ignore the fact that Clare had been crying. He made her feel important, included and welcome, immediately putting her at her ease.

'Victoria, let the kitchen staff know that I'm aiming for a seven-thirty kick-off, would you? That's to meet, not to eat.

Oh, and please let Gina and David know that I'll be around shortly. Thanks.'

He was getting Victoria out of the way. Did he know about the confrontation? In any case, he'd sensed the bad atmosphere and expertly repaired it.

'Have you all got drinks?' he asked.

'Just a new drink for Clare, please,' Kylie answered, stepping forward.

'Good to see you again, Kylie. Thank you for coming. I take it Victoria sorted out all of the arrangements?'

'Yes, we're good. You have my assurance that this entire weekend is off the record, Sebastian. Everything. I appreciate you asking me here.'

Sebastian seemed to relax when he heard those words. Matt moved closer to Clare and squeezed her hand gently. His first reaction had been to be furious with her over her outburst, but it had all been smoothed over and they could move on.

Within five minutes they were sitting around a table in the bar. Jerry had joined them from outside, their drinks were topped up and the atmosphere was genial and relaxed. Sebastian was a good host – at ease and informal, funny even. That had never really come over on TV.

Matt noticed Clare tense and he turned around to see Victoria back in the room. She whispered something into Sebastian's ear and his face became more serious. There was a commotion out on the deck, something was happening; Matt recognised the voices of Vinden and Phyllis. He could hear dogs barking. That must mean David and Gina had surfaced as well.

'We'd better go outside and meet our final guest,' Sebastian said, getting up and making it clear that everybody should follow his lead.

There were gasps of 'Wow!' and 'How daring!' A small crowd made up of the two older couples, three small yapping dogs, and Quentin and Hunter were looking up into the sky.

'Here he comes!' Vinden shouted out.

There was the drone of a small aircraft from some way off. It flew over leaving a trail of red and green smoke behind; it was lost slightly in the darkening, grey sky.

A figure was parachuting onto the deck of the fort, expertly controlling his flight path to land directly in the middle of the large white H painted in the middle of the helipad.

'Who on earth is that?' Clare gasped.

'That's Olaf Strauss!' Sebastian announced to the gathered crowd. Then muttered under his breath: 'What a prat!'

CHAPTER TEN

September, Newcastle & London, UK

It was difficult to conceal that she was job-hunting during the daytime. Clare swore Zoe to secrecy, reminding her to stay quiet on Facebook too, in case Matt spotted her posts.

The jobcentre was a depressing prospect. Clare didn't want to register as out of work, she couldn't face the grim reality of being on benefits. They'd force her into taking something she didn't want and then she'd be stuck. There were still a couple of manoeuvres that could be put in place with the bank overdraft, the credit card, missed mortgage payments and what was left of Matt's allowance for the business start-up scheme. Things were extremely precarious but she didn't want Matt distracted by the impending financial doom. He needed to get his pitch as strong as it could be. He had to succeed.

Clare's routine had always been slightly out of sync with the rest of the world. She worked late and slept late. Although she was usually home before midnight, she'd sleep in until ten o'clock, sometimes eleven. Since Matt had been working from home, he'd bring her coffee at ten, and sometimes she'd doze on for another hour. He'd join her in bed at least a couple of times a week and they'd emerge after midday flushed and sweaty. As the money problems had tightened their grip and success had begun to feel more elusive for Matt, the daytime sex had diminished and the mid-morning coffees disappeared. He knew that he was fighting for his financial survival.

After she lost her job, Clare was grateful for the lack of attention. It meant she could sneak off into town and see what was on offer. Most of the work available was of the minimum wage, coffee shop variety. She'd moved out of that into the more sophisticated restaurant scene a couple of years ago. She was determined to avoid the pensioners and terminally unemployed who frequented those places. Shop work horrified her – she had no interest in clothes, shoes or household wares.

The problem with working for Franco was that he hadn't quite got round to setting up an employee benefit scheme. There was little point seeking redundancy pay, even if she was entitled to it. Anyway, she liked Franco, she didn't want to screw him into the ground.

'You're alright!' Zoe would tease her as they nursed a coffee in one of the cafés she was so keen to avoid working in. 'Matt will be a Silicon Valley millionaire soon, and you won't have to work anymore. I'll be stuck in a place like this mopping up after some granny who's pissed herself on the chairs, and you'll be having lunch with Mark Zuckerberg or popping over to Elon Musk's for a spin in his new Tesla.'

Clare suspected that could be some way off. Matt's idea still might fail, and even if he was successful, there was a lot of demanding work ahead.

By the time the big weekend arrived, she was ready for a change of scene. She was also primed for a couple of days away from Matt. She didn't like having to deceive him all the time, it was tiring her out.

'So, you're okay? You've got your train tickets, you remembered the card and the prezzie?'

Matt always got a bit clingy before sending her off on a trip. There was something about the railway station that did it. Brief Encounter had been on to something all those years ago.

'Yes, false teeth, clean knickers and toothbrush. I'm good to go. You forgot to mention the second-class rail ticket, by the way. And then, of course, there's the bus from Lockerbie. We scum have to rough it when we travel.'

'Sebastian's picking up the tab for my trip, you know that. Besides, Moffatt isn't that far away and the air is a lot fresher than in London. And if I do get to the final round you'll be able to come along too – it'll be a weekend on one of his exclusive properties. How posh is that?'

'Here's my train.' Clare kissed Matt on the cheek. He moved his lips to her mouth and for a moment the kiss was deep and passionate. 'I'll see you on Monday. Send me a text or Facebook me or whatever works – let me know how it's going.'

Matt gave Clare a hug and picked up her bag.

'Send my love to Isabelle. Tell her I'll make it up to her when we're rich!'

They'd managed to decipher the letters painted onto the platform so they were standing directly in front of her carriage. He waved her off, and then headed over to his own platform. There was twenty minutes between their trains. He made himself a coffee in the First Class lounge and that took him up nicely to his own departure time.

He was so preoccupied with the weekend ahead that Clare left his thoughts the moment the train drew out of Newcastle station. He sat back and stretched out his legs ready enjoy the lunch that was about to be served. There was always something about travelling in First – on the rare occasions that he'd done it – that made him feel more affluent than he was.

It was a weekend of feeling that way. Slightly sloshed from the full glasses of wine poured on the train, Matt took a taxi from Kings Cross to the Magnum Hotel. It was amazing, the sort of place where they had a dedicated trolley to take your bags to your room. And the room itself had a huge double bed, the most luxurious bathrobes he'd ever seen, a substantial desk with a leather upholstered chair and a bottle of very expensive whisky to greet him. It had a handwritten tag attached to it: *See you later, enjoy the facilities, Sebastian.*

If he'd liked whisky, it would have been even better.

Clare messaged him to let him know that she'd arrived. The bus ride had been horrible, but the B&B was fine. People were starting to gather for Isabelle's wedding and she wouldn't have much time to chat. Matt sent a similar reply. He was about to shower, hadn't a clue how long the evening reception would go on, and anticipated being busy all day on the Saturday while they were working with their mentors and honing their pitches. They signed off with a *Love you x.* It would be some time before either felt they could offer that sentiment with complete sincerity.

The invitation to the reception had been clear: dress was casual, no suits required. Sebastian was a fifty-something guy who wore only T-shirts and jeans. It was his trademark look. Part of the Helix folklore was that he'd walked out of his corporate office as a younger man and swore that he'd never wear a suit and tie again. It seemed to be working well for him.

Matt had been checking out the finalists on LinkedIn. A few had fledgeling companies. There were more women than men, mirroring Sebastian's other sworn vow to guarantee that women would never have a secondary place in his organisation. He was way ahead of his time – the rest of the world was still sweating about whether their female employees would be getting pregnant anytime soon.

The truth was, Sebastian Helix seemed like a man you could trust. He had that Midas touch. So far, everything Matt had touched had turned into a turd. At least, it felt that way to him.

It didn't feel quite right walking into that room in a plain T-shirt and jeans, but Matt was relieved to see that it hadn't been a trick, and most people had adhered to the dress code. Some of the women had worn dresses, but that didn't count as breaking the rules. One young guy had come dressed in a green suit with a bright red bow tie. He was loud and arrogant.

Prat, Matt thought. *There's always someone who has to be different.*

There was plenty of alcohol on offer and a wide variety of canapés, most of which he couldn't identify, but all were delicious. He'd paced himself badly, and he'd need to stuff down the canapés to soak up the drink. He was already tipsy from his wine on the train. He didn't want to let himself down on such an important night.

He cursed himself for arriving too late. Everybody was chatting away in small huddles and it was difficult to break in. He didn't know anybody. He decided to lurk around the food area hoping that another late arrival would strike up a conversation.

'Hi, you must be Matt.'

It was a female voice, very well-modulated and sure of itself.

'I got you a drink. Hope you don't mind. You looked a bit lost on your own.'

You can say that again, Matt thought. He ran his tongue over his teeth, checking for food debris, then turned around and gave the most confident I'm-worthy-of-funding smile that he could muster.

'Hi, pleased to meet you. I'm Victoria Winterton.'

CHAPTER ELEVEN

October, Helix Fort

Olaf's arrival changed the dynamic immediately. He made himself the centre of attention. Parachuting onto a multi-millionaire's maritime fort tends to do that. The coloured smoke blowing across the deck from his canisters also helped.

Gina and David's dogs were yapping constantly and straining at their leashes. Matt rather hoped that they would savage Olaf, but knew that one kick from his boots would send all three scampering away. They were tiny, ornamental creatures.

Kylie whispered to Clare, and Matt caught what she said. It wasn't meant for his ears.

'He may be an arse, but I'd certainly take a turn. Look at the size of that guy!'

Clare seemed embarrassed. She wasn't used to making comments about men and speculating as to their suitability as a mate. However, it was quite clear to Matt that Olaf had made an immediate impact on her. Instinctively, he pulled in his stomach.

'Oh look, it's Olaf Strauss!' said Sebastian, setting aside his personal dislike and becoming the good host once again.

Olaf took off his helmet and goggles, and then removed his harness. He expertly gathered in the opened parachute and walked down the steps of the helipad towards the main deck. It seemed to Matt that he was used to drawing a crowd.

David and Gina's dogs were straining at the leash to do whatever it was that they wanted to do to Olaf's legs. In a move that Matt hadn't seen so neatly delivered since watching a Doctor Doolittle cartoon as a youngster, Olaf knelt down and started to talk to them softly.

'Hey, little guys. It's only me, Olaf!'

They were silenced instantly.

'What now! He's the bloody Dog Whisperer.'

Matt turned to Clare, hoping she'd share in the joke, but she was too busy checking out Olaf. He'd never seen her salivate so openly in the presence of another man. She'd never drooled over him like that. He felt immediately proprietorial. Kylie was as bad – and it looked like even Phyllis was ready to cast aside her menopausal flushes and take her turn.

Matt hated Olaf Strauss. He was one of those guys who was born with an easy charm and an instant likableness. The bastard. And he was a prick.

Having calmed the dogs and won David and Gina's immediate respect, Olaf stood in front of the group and unzipped his overalls. Underneath, he was wearing skimpy Speedos, which left very little to the imagination.

'Who's coming to join me in the hot tub?'

He looked across at Clare and Kylie. It was as if he knew Clare's number one aim was to get into that tub, and now here was an Adonis offering to make her wish come true. They were giggling like schoolgirls being paid attention by the school's rugby captain. But it was Phyllis who piped up first.

'You bet, young man! I love a session in the hot tub.'

Her face reddened, and it wasn't a menopausal flush. Olaf appeared to have resurrected impulses in her which looked like they might have been out of bounds to Vinden for some time. Vinden looked put out.

Olaf picked up his kit and thrust it at Eddy. Matt saw Eddy tense, instantly clenching his fist, and then just as quickly unclenching it. His face relaxed as he reached out to accept the pile of discarded gear.

'I take it my cases arrived on the boat?' Olaf asked to nobody in particular.

'Yes, Mr Strauss,' Eddy replied. 'Everything has been placed in your room.'

'Before you all head off to the tub, I have a couple of announcements to make about the weekend. As Olaf has succeeded in bringing us all together, now seems like an opportune moment.'

Sebastian was wrestling back control from his newly arrived guest.

'There are a few things I need to mention,' he began.

Clare was like a passenger on an aeroplane during the safety announcements. She was pretending to listen, but her attention was elsewhere. She couldn't keep her eyes off Olaf's body. He was perfectly toned, with the type of six-pack that Matt had only seen on magazine models – and those he'd always assumed to be computer-generated. It turned out he was wrong about that. Olaf's body was completely hairless, waxed to within an inch of its life, his manhood barely contained in the skimpiest, tightest briefs that he'd ever seen. However cold it had been when making the jump from the light aircraft, it appeared not to have made any impact on Olaf. Matt, on the other hand, had retreated to the safety of baggy swimwear some years ago.

'The evening's entertainment will begin at half-seven,' Sebastian continued. 'I have brought along Yves, my personal chef, who will be working with a small team of waiting staff to take care of your every need. Other than that, Eddy and Victoria are here to deal with any problems. Feel free to roam where you please, out of bounds areas are clearly marked for your personal safety.'

'You remembered that I'm a vegan, yeah?' asked Olaf. Of course he was. It would be no weekend with Olaf Strauss if he didn't have to have a special menu option. 'We don't want to scare off these little fellas, do we?' he said, stroking one of the dogs and smiling at Gina.

They'd be quite happy to take a chunk out of you, if they were hungry enough, thought Matt, but kept the quip to himself. He didn't feel as if he'd have a sympathetic audience if he started taking potshots at Olaf.

'Yes, we have vegan food for you, Olaf, and a coeliac menu for Vinden, no problem at all. I ought to warn you that the weather is forecast to get a little rough overnight and on Saturday, but we'll be clear to leave at our designated time on Sunday afternoon. During the severe weather, we won't be able to sail or to fly, so you have a narrow window of opportunity if you wish to leave for any reason. But, of course, I hope that you'll stay and enjoy your time on Helix Fort this weekend and that we'll also have an excellent few days of business together.'

There was a round of applause from the gathered guests, and several cheers of 'Well done, Seb!' and 'Wonderful, what a splendid host!' from those who were already familiar with this level of hospitality.

'One last thing,' he continued, after the excitement died down. 'Many of you will be aware that Matt and Olaf here are finalists in my Global Entrepreneur Challenge. Both gentlemen will be spending time with me in the conference room as I make the final decision about whom I'll be funding. Please excuse my absence from some events while we conduct that business. However, I will take immense pleasure in joining you for a special banquet on Saturday evening, when I will announce the winner. I hope you will all make my other guests welcome – Matt's lovely wife, Clare, and Kylie Parker of CelebUK magazine, who joins us this weekend as my personal guest rather than as a journalist.'

Matt watched as Olaf checked out Clare. Knowing that she was Matt's wife had made her immediately more attractive to him, whether he fancied her or not. He grinned at Matt when he saw he was being watched. It was the sort of challenge that you'd get from one of the sports team guys at school, as if to say, *Why would she look twice at you, dickhead, when I'm here?*

'As usual, what happens on the fort stays on the fort – even more so this weekend with Kylie's notebook tightly under lock and key!'

There was some polite laughter, and then Sebastian concluded his speech.

'What's mine is yours this weekend. Please help yourself to everything that's on offer. If you have anything – and

I mean anything – that's bothering you, please speak to Victoria or Eddy. We'll meet in the former mess hall for a special welcome meal at half-past seven this evening. In the meantime, have a great weekend!'

Olaf looked as if he had every intention of helping himself to everything that was on offer. There was another round of applause for Sebastian, and the group began to disperse. Ever alert to where the focus of attention was resting, Olaf piped up immediately.

'Last one into the hot tub fetches the drinks!'

Clare and Kylie looked at each other and smiled.

'Hey Matt, I hope you'll be joining us. I'm dying to catch up. And I want to get to know your beautiful wife. You did bring your swimming things?'

Matt was about to lie. He couldn't face the humiliation of having to climb into a hot tub with Olaf. The man had complete physical superiority.

'Yes, we brought our swimming suits,' Clare answered for him. She didn't consider for one moment that he might not want to join them.

'Okay then, I'll see you in there. You coming too, Phyllis?'

'I wouldn't miss it!'

She abandoned Vinden to rush off to her room to get changed.

'Come on!' said Kylie. 'You heard what Sebastian said – the weather might force us inside tomorrow. Best get our kit off as soon as possible!'

'You coming?' Clare turned to Matt, her face the most enthusiastic that he'd seen it for a long time. 'You did say that you'd try the hot tub.'

Matt saw there was no way he was getting out of it. He

made one last attempt to retain his dignity, but Clare was having none of it.

'You need to be careful with Olaf. He's a bit of a womaniser. He doesn't always keep his hands to himself.'

Then the killer blow.

'What, like you were careful with Victoria Winterton? Sure, I'll take that kind of care. No problem.'

CHAPTER TWELVE

October, Helix Fort

The hot tub was an excruciating experience for Matt. If it wasn't for Vinden's liver-spotted, saggy old body covered from head to toe in straggly grey hairs, there would have been no consolation for him whatsoever. Vinden had made the decision to follow Phyllis into the tub rather than be left to his own devices. He'd opted for humiliation, too.

Olaf was doing stretching exercises by the time he and Clare emerged on the deck. Of course he was. Nothing was left to the imagination.

Clare was in a skimpy one-piece and Kylie had brought along a bikini. They looked hot, in great shape, completely at ease alongside Olaf. Phyllis had just about managed to squeeze everything into her swimming suit, although whether it would stay there was doubtful. There was an unspoken understanding that, while he would flirt with Phyllis, Kylie and Clare were the only women that were really in play for Olaf.

As the five of them got into the pool, Matt sucked in his stomach, pulled up his shorts and made his way self-consciously up to the side of the tub. Olaf was already laughing with Clare and Kylie, two intelligent women turned to jelly by the presence of this good-looking oaf.

Olaf let Matt lower himself into the water before dropping his next bombshell.

'Hey, Matt, you were last in the tub. You get to fetch the drinks!'

As Matt stood up, his shorts, pulled down by the weight of the water, dropped below the crack of his butt and he was forced to hoist them up as Clare and Kylie laughed at his discomfort. He suspected that Clare was getting her own back on him. If she was, she was being a cow. It wasn't necessary, he knew what he'd done.

Dripping and shivering with cold, he waddled over to the bar. They'd agreed to load up with random cocktails, and he asked the barman to fill up a tray with whatever he thought best. They exchanged pleasantries as the cocktails were being made, and Matt was painfully aware of how unattractive his own body had become. His small paunch hung over his waistband, his chest wobbled every time he moved, and hair was beginning to grow in places that it had never thought of before. He was still in his early thirties; he'd always thought he wouldn't be troubled by such indignities until later in life.

Looking across to Olaf and the way that he commanded the attention of everybody around him – his wife included – Matt felt suddenly vulnerable. He'd been with Clare so long, he'd never thought her capable of having her attention diverted from the marriage. He'd worked and worked to get his idea off the ground, and the gym memberships had lapsed and the inactivity had crept in.

'Come and swim with me at the city pool,' she'd urged. 'It's really cheap and it'll keep you in decent shape.'

Matt had declined, choosing instead to spend more hours coding at his computer.

As he dripped onto the thick carpeting in the bar, he realised that if he didn't pull off the deal over the weekend he'd have to move fast to put things right. He had no money, no job and was going to seed. The thought of losing Clare was a torment to him. He wanted her to join him in this new world of rock stars and entrepreneurs, not move out of his life. Looking at her in that hot tub – confident, sexy, fun, alive – he wondered if he was the problem, not Clare.

Returning with the tray of drinks, Matt made a clumsy attempt to wrestle the focus from Olaf. It immediately backfired. He was out of his depth.

'Who's up for Sex on the Beach?' he asked, as playfully as he could manage.

'Well, I certainly don't fancy your Slippery Nipple!' Olaf laughed.

Matt tensed his chest to stop his newly grown moobs shaking, but it was too late. Everybody had looked up at him and was joining in the laughter. Except for Clare who, just for a second, looked like she was going to leap to her husband's defence. He wished there was a drink called Oily Snake, but that one hadn't been invented yet.

'Hey, Matt!' Olaf said, sipping his newly delivered cocktail. 'Did you know that Helix is going to try to pitch for IP? That's why he got us here without any lawyers around.'

This seemed to be a sensible conversation at last, but Matt was embarrassed that he didn't know what Olaf was talking about.

'What do you mean?' asked Clare.

She didn't know it, but she'd just helped him to save face.

'IP stands for intellectual property. Usually you get angel funding – that's where rich people support your idea with their own money and mentorship, like on Dragon's Den. They ask for a percentage of the business. But I reckon he's going to request intellectual property rights – he wants it all.'

This is where Phyllis and Vinden were back on terra firma. When it came to matters of money and investment, the liver spots and uneven deposits of fat faded into insignificance.

'Surrendering intellectual property rights isn't a good idea,' said Vinden. 'IP is where the true value resides. I don't know what kind of offer Seb is planning to make you, but that seems unlikely. He's not a shark-like that.'

'Well, I have a friend in tech who says it's how it always plays out,' Olaf replied. 'He'll make a cash offer, which will seem fab to someone like Matt who won't read the small print. Buyer beware, my friend. Buyer beware.'

Matt couldn't believe that Olaf would for one minute be prepared to share any advice which might help him on his way to making a better business decision. And in any case, at that moment he'd have been willing to exchange his big idea for a year's salary and the chance to pay off his debts, but there was no way he was admitting that to Olaf.

The mood changed again as Olaf discovered a plastic duck tucked away to the side of the hot tub.

'Quack, quack!' he said, chasing Kylie and Clare through the water, the tomfoolery getting more physical by the minute.

Matt had had enough. He couldn't watch any longer.

'I'm getting out for a coffee.'

He made sure he'd adjusted his waistband properly before he stood up. Kylie looked at Clare who was laughing at Olaf's antics. It made Matt feel boring and bland.

'I'll come with you. I could murder a coffee!'

Was she playing wingman to Clare? Surely Kylie wouldn't encourage a dangerous game like that right under his nose?

'Enjoy yourselves, party-poopers!' Clare called out as they walked across the deck to the bar.

It was a long time since Matt had seen her like that. He was jealous of Olaf Strauss. It was hard to admit it, but he was insanely envious of the man. Knowing his luck, Strauss would win the competition then steal his wife. Just the thought of it felt physically painful.

'She loves you, you know,' said Kylie. 'She knows that Olaf is a tosser – we both do. She's trying to get your attention.'

Matt was prickly with his answer, and he immediately regretted it.

'I didn't realise marriage guidance was part of the deal this weekend.'

'Woah, steady on. I'm trying to help here. She knows what she's doing. She's trying to make you jealous. Men like Olaf are just eye-candy. Any woman knows they're not husband material.'

'Well, she's doing an excellent job on the jealousy front,' Matt replied. 'And you could have fooled me about the messing around. She looks like she could eat him alive.'

'She's only playing. She's entitled to after what you did, isn't she?'

'How do you know—'

'I was there on the night. I saw what you did. Victoria Winterton had you in her sights from the get-go.'

'What exactly did you see?'

'Does it matter? You know what you did. Clare's a lovely girl, Matt. Don't mess it up, not with you on the verge of getting a deal with Sebastian.'

The coffees arrived. Matt was relieved, he was getting cold. He pushed the patio door shut, not only to keep the warm in but also to shut out the sound of laughter from his wife. The patio heaters were effective on the deck, but the door was best closed when inside the bar area.

'No really, what did you see? Because I'm not entirely sure what actually happened.'

'I wasn't watching you all night, but you seemed to be getting on very well. I remember her laughing and touching you. First your arm, then your hand. And I remember you leaving most clearly. She was holding your hand. But you know that already.'

Matt studied Kylie's face. He was sitting opposite a beautiful young woman in a very revealing swimsuit and he'd only just realised it. He really was getting old or, at least, beginning to behave that way.

'I don't recall a lot about that night - I'd had too much to drink.'

'Don't even think about trying on that old excuse. I hope that's not what you told Clare. She hasn't told me exactly what she knows, but I can put two and two together. You really upset her. You've broken her heart.'

When Matt had signed up for this weekend retreat, he'd been looking forward to relaxing in amazing company with lots of engaging conversation. He'd barely been there a couple of hours and already his best mate, Riff, had abandoned him to his fate in the hot tub. His smart-arse of an opponent in the funding contest had wowed everybody with a stunning entrance and was now splashing in a warm pool with his wife. And here he was, shivering in a bar and taking relationship advice from her new buddy, while Clare got cosy with a man who quite clearly wanted to sleep with her. It wasn't at all what he'd envisaged.

'Seriously, Matt, you could walk away with a fabulous offer this weekend. I'm certainly hoping to do likewise. This is life-changing money. You've seen how screwed Jerry and Sebastian have been by their marital break-ups. Make sure you and Clare aren't next.'

The timing was perfect. As Kylie finished speaking, Victoria Winterton stepped into the bar to give him the nod that it was time for a quick one-to-one chat with Sebastian.

'Fifteen minutes,' she warned. 'Just time for a shower, if you want one. Will you let Olaf know? You'll get half an hour for this session, and then he'll be next. Following that, we eat in the mess hall.'

'Of course!' said Matt, getting up to give Clare a shout from the patio door. Any excuse to interrupt whatever was going on outside. As he turned towards the hot tub, he noticed that things had quietened down a little since he'd last looked. Clare was pulling up the strap on her swimsuit while Olaf used his hand to guide her wet hair out of her eyes.

CHAPTER THIRTEEN

September, London, UK

Matt was pleased to have Victoria there. She seemed happy to talk to him, and he was relieved that he was no longer a spare part at the reception. Everybody seemed to be so much more confident than he was.

He'd been chatting away to her when there was a sudden explosion of light and sound and Sebastian Helix walked onto a small stage surrounded by promotional pull-ups sporting the Helix logo and brands. The showbiz was splendid, but he'd expect nothing less from one of the UK's best-known entrepreneurs.

'Good evening, ladies and gentlemen. I'm Richard Branson!'

There was a loud roar of laughter. The two men were often compared, but Helix was generally a tech-guy, he didn't do trains or bank accounts.

Matt was aware of a laugh that was more distinctive

than the others, it stood out and drew his ear. It was the man in the green suit. That made sense.

'Seriously though folks, I'm really Alan Sugar and you're all fired!'

Another roar of laughter, and this time when it had subsided the man in the green suit could still be heard making enthusiastic whooping sounds.

'Who let that chimpanzee into the room?' Helix joked, immediately aware that he had a jerk in the crowd. The comment was enough to silence the noises, at least for a brief time.

'I'd like to welcome our ten finalists here this evening and congratulate you for getting this far. Whether you leave empty-handed or not this weekend, you are all remarkable people and you should be extremely proud of what you've achieved.'

There was a round of applause, this time for themselves. Green suit man decided to tone it down a bit.

'I'd like you to take the time to get to know each other this evening and to speak to the mentors who are also among you. We have some members of the press here too – feel free to chat with them if you wish. Tomorrow we'll reconvene in here at 10 o'clock sharp and you'll be asked to move around the mentors in a speed-dating style session. In the afternoon, we'll run breakouts and eight of you will be eliminated ...'

There was a moment of suspense while they waited for Helix's next words.

'... but don't worry, we'll still pay your rail fare back home!'

More laughter, relieved laughter this time. The man in the green suit was back again, his wings only temporarily clipped.

'Please, in the meantime, enjoy yourselves, tuck into the food and drink and get to know each other. Tomorrow we work hard and, by the close of play on Sunday, two of you will be so close to the funding prize that you'll be able to smell the money!'

There was a huge cheer, another round of applause, and then Sebastian moved off the stage. The initial groupings were now disrupted, and it was musical chairs as everybody sought a new conversation to cling to. Victoria had disappeared.

Matt worked his way around the crowd, mixing with mentors and fellow entrepreneurs. Everything was beginning to swim around him as the alcohol worked its way through his body and the room became more stuffy and overheated.

Everywhere he went, he was aware of the man in the green suit. He seemed to be on intimate terms with everybody in the room. It turned out that he was one of the other contestants: Olaf Strauss. Matt knew the name and he was disappointed to see who it belonged to. How could a man with such an amazing concept be such a loudmouth? He could only steer away from him for so long before it became impossible to avoid him.

'Hey, you're Matt Dalton, aren't you? Pleased to meet you, man. If it wasn't for you, I'd have this in the bag.'

Olaf stretched out his hand. His handshake was unnecessarily firm and Matt's hand was quite sore once he'd finally released his grasp. He decided to play nice.

'Well, your idea is pretty amazing. That's astonishing if you can really deliver that level of battery life in a smartphone. You must feel like you've got the world at your feet.'

'Yeah, pretty well. It's good for pussy too, if you know

what I mean, my friend. I won't be going away empty-handed this weekend, that's for sure.'

He cupped his hands as if he was caressing breasts to illustrate his point, on the off chance it had been missed.

Matt recoiled. He'd done nothing to invite that level of familiarity and crassness.

'I'd rather you didn't use that kind of language around me,' he said, determined to stand his ground. Idiots were always saying inappropriate things to Clare at her work, and this sort of behaviour had to be challenged.

He was stunned at Olaf's response. It was the opposite of the contriteness he'd anticipated.

'Wow, man, you're rather over-sensitive, aren't you? No need to be completely humourless. It's not a funeral, you know!'

People were watching now. Olaf was speaking loudly and Matt's face was reddening. Then he completely blindsided Matt by knocking his glass of juice out of his hand. It went flying all over the dress of one of the mentors chatting in a group to the side of them. Fanning the flames of the commotion, Olaf suggested that Matt might be a little worse for wear.

Matt was furious. He apologised to the woman, and she left the room in a hurry to clean herself up. He tried to help the staff clear up the mess, but by the time Olaf was finished, even Matt was blaming himself for having drunk too much.

He was relieved when Victoria came over to rescue him.

'Don't worry about it. Seriously, that man is an idiot. I saw what happened. He knocked your glass.'

She touched him on the arm reassuringly.

'It won't have scuppered my chances with Sebastian, will it?'

'He wasn't even here, he's had to leave the room to deal with some business matters. He didn't see it. But, between you and me, he knows what Olaf is like. He tolerates him because, although he's a prat, he's a prat with an amazing product concept.'

'I'm sorry for causing any trouble, really I am. Do you mind if I get a coffee? I'd like to clear my head.'

'Good idea!' Victoria replied, touching his hand. 'I tell you what, let's go and sit on comfy chairs outside for a while. I'll get the coffees, you take a seat.'

Matt nodded. He felt exhausted by the emotional energy he'd just used. Victoria had made him feel better about it, but he still felt like an idiot. He wanted to punch Olaf.

Within five minutes, he was drinking a black coffee and chatting to Victoria in the reception area. She was funny and entertaining. She may not have been his type, but he could see how attractive she was.

A reporter by the name of Kylie Parker had also left the reception alongside them, and had taken up a position across the room from them to check her phone messages. Matt glanced up every now and then and saw how she was standing there for some time, engrossed in her phone and occasionally looking over at them.

Then came a raucous laugh. Matt's attention was drawn by the arsehole in the green suit, Olaf Strauss, his arm around two younger women. He was heading upstairs to his room.

Before he knew it, Matt, feeling drowsy, was being led by the hand up the stairs by Victoria Winterton, Sebastian Helix's PA. And in his woozy state, the last person he noticed before he headed upstairs, was a man later introduced as Eddy Simmonds who was standing at the end of the bar, watching everything.

CHAPTER FOURTEEN

October, Helix Fort

'I'm going in to meet Seb,' Matt said, unable to shake off the image of what he thought he'd just seen going on in the hot tub. 'I'll be half an hour, then it's your turn, Olaf.'

All he could think was how much he'd like to boot the smirking little shit off the side of the fort. It might not have been so bad if they weren't the two finalists. He had to keep things as cordial as possible until a winner was announced. After that, he'd never have to speak to the idiot again. As for his wife – she didn't appear to share his misgivings.

'That's cool, man. Good luck in there with Seb!'

Olaf stood up in the hot tub, the warm water running off his perfectly toned six-pack. Not for the first time, Matt pulled in his stomach, painfully aware that he'd begun to let himself go.

'Hey, Clare, what do you say we visit the sauna before we have to call it a day? There's nothing quite like it. You ever tried one?'

'I haven't been in a sauna for years. We've got half an hour before Matt's finished with Seb. Let's do it!'

Clare was behaving as if she'd forgotten that she was married. Was she doing it to spite him? Matt didn't know, but if that's what her aim was, it was working.

Clare stood up in the hot tub. She was stunning in her swimsuit. Matt had been busy for so long that he'd stopped noticing.

Almost forgetting him in her impatience to get to the sauna, she returned and gave him a peck on the cheek.

'Good luck! Give it your best shot!'

Off she rushed with Olaf. As they ran along the deck, dripping water behind them, Olaf reached out to take Clare's hand on the pretence of making sure she didn't slip. She had the decency to brush it away while Matt was watching. Matt wanted to lock Olaf in the steam room on his own for two hours until he emerged looking like a shriv-elled prune.

Instead, he waited for the sauna door to close, locking in shrieks of laughter. He and Clare hadn't laughed like that for a long time. But, angry as he was, he still trusted her. She was no pushover. If Olaf had written her off as another foolish woman who'd instantly fall for his sculptured body and easy humour, he was mistaken. Clare might have been angry with him – she had good reason to be, he was angry enough with himself – but Matt knew, when push came to shove, Clare was faithful. She wasn't that kind of woman.

He turned away and began to walk to the bar. Kylie was there, she'd been watching.

'That little prick Olaf should piss off. You need to let Clare know that you care about her. Don't let her slip through your fingers.'

Matt nodded and made his way back to his room. Being

circular, it was difficult to get properly lost on the fort, but it was still easy to get disorientated. He hadn't clocked it previously, but all the bedrooms were labelled with the names of Sebastian's businesses and services. He knew that he and Clare were in the Phonetica suite, but he hadn't placed that in context. There was also the Mazadrill suite and the Zimella suite; it was a history of Sebastian Helix's apps and software services. Matt wondered if his concept would ever end up on one of those doors. The thought of it was intoxicating.

He let himself into the room. Something felt immediately different, but he couldn't work out what it was. He scanned the bed, the desk, the cases. He hadn't taken any notice of where things had been placed, but he was as sure as he could be that somebody had been in the room. He thought back to the hot tub. Had Clare nipped back to get a towel perhaps? No, there were towels provided on the deck, Clare hadn't been back in the room. He opened his case and felt in the toe of his second pair of shoes. It was still there, the pen drive.

Had Olaf been sneaking around the room trying to get detailed information about his idea? He was an A-hole, but would he go that far? Surely not. He'd have to have a quiet word with Eddy. Olaf had over-stepped the mark if this was his work.

Matt needed a better place to hide the pen drive. He looked around the bedroom, wondering where might be safe. After considering several possible hiding places, he lucked out by finding a tiny tear in the mattress. He inserted the pen drive into the lining and covered it with the sheets to throw any unwelcome intruders off the scent. That bloody Olaf Strauss. Not content with stealing his wife, he also wanted to sneak a look at his project too.

He'd got the second part of his project information stored in the cloud, so even if somebody did get their hands on the pen drive they'd still only have half of what they needed. He knew its value, he wasn't stupid.

By the time he'd finished checking around the bedroom, he was short of time. He showered quickly, towelled his hair, put on jeans and a clean shirt and hastily made his way up to the conference room, notes under his arm. Outside the door he took a deep breath. This was it, he was entering the final round. By the time he left Helix Fort, he'd know if he was walking away empty-handed or not. He knocked.

'Come in!' came Sebastian's voice.

Victoria was in there with him. They were sitting together looking over some notes. Matt felt his face reddening, and he noticed that Victoria was blushing too.

'Ah, Matt, great to see you. Thanks for coming. This is an informal chat before the weekend proper starts. No need to panic. It isn't part of the final decision. I wanted to get you and Olaf on your own to make sure that you're fine with everything that's going to happen over the next two days.'

He nodded to Victoria, and she took the cue, bundling up the papers and leaving the room. It was set out as a boardroom, with chairs around an obviously expensive wooden table, a projector, screen and flipchart: the essential components of every boring corporate meeting that has ever taken place. Even Sebastian Helix couldn't escape the horrors of PowerPoint. His greatest service to man would be to invent an alternative. He could leave the trivial mosquito research to people like Bill Gates.

'Come closer, Matt. I don't bite!'

Matt had positioned himself as if he were about to be interviewed. Sebastian indicated that he should take Victoria's recently vacated chair. She'd left it warm for him.

'How are you getting on with Olaf? He's a bit of a challenge, isn't he?'

'You could say that!' Matt said with a smile.

Much as he hated Olaf, he didn't want to be seen to stab his competitor in the back, not as far as the Global Entrepreneur Challenge was concerned. When it came to his wife, however, he'd cheerfully punch the man in the face.

'He's a clever guy though, and he's going to take some beating.'

Sebastian nodded. Matt would place money on his not getting a similarly diplomatic answer from Olaf if he was asked the same question.

'Look Matt, I'm not going to beat around the bush. This conversation is off the record – it doesn't go beyond these four walls, okay?'

Matt hadn't expected this. Sebastian's tone had changed, quite suddenly. Was this how rich guys did business?

'I know this weekend is under the guise of a competition, but frankly it doesn't matter what the outcome is. The entire purpose of the thing is for me to fast-track great ideas and bring them to market as soon as possible. You have a great idea and no ability whatsoever to bring it to market. A clever idea is worth nothing if you have no means of delivering it. Am I right?'

Matt felt he was talking to a different man. This wasn't the genial Sebastian Helix who inappropriately sprayed champagne over scantily dressed models while launching his latest app project. This was an altogether different person. He'd changed almost as suddenly as Dr Jekyll and Mr Hyde.

Matt moved his head, but it was neither a nod nor a

shake. He had no ability to bring his product to market on his own. Of course he hadn't, but he wasn't going to acknowledge it in front of the man whose money he wanted.

'Quite frankly, Olaf's idea is far more promising and will make me much more money. I want to buy you out here and now, at a fair price. I have the legal paperwork ready. You can sign it right now and your financial worries will be over – you'll be able to clear all your debts.'

Matt didn't know what to say or how to react. He went for the poker-face option, while frantically thinking things over. Was this a test? Was Helix testing how serious Matt was about the whole thing? And how the hell did he know about his money worries? Had Clare told him?

'Go on,' Matt said. It was the best he could do. He needed thinking time.

'Here's my offer – I won't make it again: two hundred thousand pounds for the full IP and a one-year consultancy contract for you to support the transition to my team. We'll pay you another 75k for your year's work. It'll be a couple of meetings in London and some Skype calls. After that you're done. Easy money. What do you say?'

Matt added it up. That would clear the debts, pay off the mortgage and buy a new car. It would give him a year to breathe, and they could sort themselves out, maybe even start that family they'd been talking about.

But this was his big play, his amazing idea. Delivered correctly, it could make a fortune, and here was Sebastian Helix making a bargain-basement offer. But Helix had the infrastructure to make it happen, while Matt had neither the skills nor the financial resilience to get the idea out there.

'Can I think about it?'

A losing idea was worth nothing at all. He could leave Helix Fort empty-handed on Sunday, and then where would he be? Broke, struggling to get his marriage back on track and hugely disappointed. He wasn't certain if he could face that prospect.

'No,' Sebastian replied. 'It's a one-time offer. I can transfer the money right now if you sign the paperwork. Two hundred thousand direct to your bank account – all your troubles will be over. It's up to you. If you walk away now, you know what you're up against with Olaf. The man may be a prick, but that breakthrough of his is a licence to print money. The choice is yours. You need to make your mind up.'

CHAPTER FIFTEEN

October, Helix Fort

'Did you really need to behave like that earlier in the hot tub? I know you're angry with me, but seriously? You looked like a couple of those fools you see on Love Island.'

Clare carried on working through her dress choices for the evening. Matt hadn't told her about the meeting with Sebastian, brushing it off as a briefing session ahead of the main weekend presentations. He wasn't ready to tell her what he'd done yet.

'What do you think, something revealing for Olaf?' she hissed at him. Then a moment of silence and an apology. 'I'm sorry. I'm just so furious about Victoria Winterton being here. You must realise I think Olaf is a prat. He's fun, but it's like messing around with an eighteen-year-old. He's hardly subtle.'

Matt didn't mention what he thought he'd seen going on in the tub earlier. Had anything worse happened in the sauna? He had to put it aside and trust her. They needed to ease this tension between them so they could put on a united front at the evening meal. The edges of their relationship were fraying; they had to stop picking at the threads and put an end to the unravelling.

'I can't tell you enough times, Clare. I don't know what happened that night. I don't fancy Victoria. I must have been drunk – it's unforgivable, I know. I'll make it up to you, I promise.'

'I'm going to wear this one, alright?'

Matt nodded. It was a simple, plain, long black dress. Always classy and completely safe in any company.

He checked his mobile phone again. There was still no signal. It could stay in the room for the evening.

'I hate to think how everybody else will be dressed now the jeans and shirts are out of the way. Have you seen the jewellery this lot are wearing? And that's when we're mixing informally, we haven't even got to the posh bit yet!'

'Clare, you look beautiful to me just as you are.'

He meant every word of it. Matt thought she looked stunning. Over sixteen years together and she could still take his breath away. Feeling the threat from Olaf had made him appreciate what he'd got. He'd felt pure jealousy out there on the deck.

'Are you really going like that?' Clare asked, brushing off the compliment, but pleased that he'd said it. 'I think a jacket would be good, even without a tie.'

'*Formally informal* the briefing said,' Matt replied, 'so I take that to mean no jeans. Anyway, you wait and see what Olaf turns up in. He'll be making a statement in some way.'

'Still, wear a jacket, please,' Clare urged. 'Besides, it's quite cold outside, you might be grateful for it later.'

Matt obliged. He didn't have the energy to argue over the little things.

'Shall we go for a walk on deck before eating?' Clare suggested. 'It might help to calm my nerves.'

They both knew that the bickering had to stop. They had to present a united front for the evening. Besides, nobody wants to spend time with a quarrelling couple.

The deck area was well screened from the wind and the patio heaters were burning fiercely, but Matt was immediately grateful for his jacket. Clare had learned her lesson from stepping out of the helicopter earlier, and knew to restrict her movements to the sheltered areas. This was an important night and it was essential that her hair stayed in place for the meal. It was dark now and the wind was howling beyond the fort. They moved to a covered area draped in fairy lights and surrounded by well-tended plants in huge tubs. They'd hoped to see the lights of the shore, but the visibility was too poor. The waves crashed below them. It was both dramatic and impressive.

'I can see why Sebastian bought this place,' Clare began, choosing to stick to safe topics. 'What a way to escape the world. I've never seen anything like it.'

They sensed movement to their side and looked up. It was Eddy. He was up on the circular platform of the lighthouse, walking around, looking out in different directions.

'Probably having a crafty cigarette,' Matt commented. 'It must be blowing a gale up there. The things you have to do for a fag these days.'

'Did you hear that?' Clare asked.

'What?'

'Voices. And there's an engine sound from somewhere too.'

'Is that the generator? You get used to it after a while.'

'No, move to the side. It's out at sea, I'm certain.'

Matt repositioned himself and listened.

'You're right, there's definitely a different engine sound out there. And I did hear a voice. It could be a fishing boat. I saw a ferry pass by earlier – the fort must be on a shipping lane. Sebastian said the weather was going to be bad tonight. I wouldn't want to be out in it.'

'It must be very close if we can hear it,' Clare observed.

'I'm no Captain Birdseye, but I'm guessing that's what the lighthouse must be for, to stop anything crashing into us. We're so close to Portsmouth that there must be boats of all sizes in and out of this area all the time. Wasn't this fort built in the nineteenth century to defend us from the French? It must be in some nautically advantageous position. But, as I said, I'm no Captain Birdseye, I assume you have to stick a lighthouse on top of something like this if it's in the middle of the sea?'

Clare laughed. It was good to hear. It was not as easy a laugh as it had been with Olaf, but it was a start, a glimpse of how they used to be.

'Yes, probably.'

Clare closed off the conversation as suddenly as she'd started it. They were no longer alone. Quentin and Hunter had joined them on the deck.

'Hi guys,' said Quentin.

Both men were immaculately dressed in evening wear. Matt immediately saw that he'd made the wrong decision about his clothing choices.

'Come to take the air before the tour?'

'Yes, though it's a bit wild out here, isn't it?' said Clare, giving Matt an *I told you so* look.

'What's the form at these events? Have you been before?' Matt asked, self-conscious now.

'You know Seb. Anything goes really, but we like to

dress up, although we've only done this once before. We're newbies like you.'

Clare thought that Hunter might have been crying. His voice sounded reedy, as if he was testing it out before he had to use it for real in the dining area.

'Besides,' Quentin chipped in, 'you've seen that Olaf guy. It wouldn't surprise me if he makes his entrance looking like Priscilla, Queen of the Desert!'

The laughter helped to break the awkwardness. What do you say to a couple of TV celebrities? Resting TV celebrities, come to that. Quentin helped to make things easier for everybody.

'You know they're all gossiping about us, don't you? And you must have read all the articles about us?'

Clare nodded. Matt wondered what was coming.

'Well, to set the story straight so that everybody knows the truth: yes, we did get sacked. No, we're not splitting up. And, fingers crossed, we are going to sail away from this place with a couple of contracts and maybe even a new TV format.'

'Wow!' said Clare, a little taken aback by the barrage of news headlines. 'It sounds like you have a lot resting on this visit.'

'We all do, my darling,' Hunter said. 'He's gathered a little bunch of wounded creatures here this weekend. We all need something from him in one way or another. There are a lot of desperate people on Helix Fort, all needing to get their hands on their share of Sebastian's fortune.'

He laughed uncomfortably. But he was right. Matt wondered what life must be like for Sebastian with so many people wanting to feed from his financial veins. He was the same, so was Olaf. They all needed Helix's cash. They were no better than the rest of them, taking their turn in the queue, waiting for whatever hand-out they could get.

'I'm pleased to hear that you're staying together,' Matt picked up. 'It's a good thing if you can work out your differences.'

He looked at Clare, but she averted her eyes.

'We're not out of the long grass yet, but I think we'll get there,' Hunter said, squeezing Quentin's arm.

'We'd better move inside,' Quentin suggested, moving away. 'We don't want to turn up late. I hear this tour of the fort is something special – it's access to all areas.'

The party of four moved towards the entrance to the bar. Already, several of the guests were gathered there, drinks in hand, making polite chitchat.

'I told you to dress smarter,' Clare whispered to Matt, falling just behind Quentin and Hunter so that she could scold him.

The wealth on show was immense. Clare felt as plain and as penniless as she was. It looked like a pop-up jewellery shop – Phyllis and Gina seemed to be having a competition to see who could display the most wealth. Even Matt, who tended to be less affected by such things, slipped his cheap Casio watch into his pocket. He had to keep reminding himself that everybody in the room had been like him and Clare once.

The men too – Jerry, Vinden and David – gave off an aroma of extreme wealth, though the clues were harder to spot: the occasional glimpse of a watch peeping out from a shirt sleeve, jewelled cuff links catching the light and the smell of aftershave which had definitely not been purchased from Superdrug. Every little touch was a blow to Matt, reminding him that he didn't belong here, that these were not his people. Clare seemed immediately uncomfortable again, however much the women tried to put her at her ease.

'You look gorgeous, my dear. I wish to God that I were forty years younger and still had your stunning figure!'

Gina was making a real effort to be kind, but Clare knew what she was – an out-of-work waitress with a husband who was desperately trying to keep a dream of fame and fortune alive. At best, they were living on a wing and prayer. Ironically, Jerry's band had had a hit single with a song of the same name: *On a wing and a prayer*. She could picture him in the famous video, a much younger man carrying a lot less weight, playing the amazing guitar solo that accompanied the song.

They simply couldn't compete in that room. They had nothing to offer.

But within the next four hours that would all change. The wealth would count for nothing. And Matt and Clare would become the most important people on the fort that night.

CHAPTER SIXTEEN

September, London, UK

Matt had trouble coming round the next day. He couldn't shake off a terrible fatigue. He was usually good in the mornings, particularly since he'd been working for himself. Self-employment had provided a good incentive for getting up early. Every minute wasted in bed was a lost opportunity to be earning – that was the way of the aspiring entrepreneur.

He was disorientated for a few minutes. The curtains were open, it was getting light outside, but was still that in-between stage where it was neither daylight nor darkness. He took in the detail of the room. A high ceiling. A blue bedspread. He was naked – unusual, he preferred boxers and a T-shirt, even in summer. The door to the room clicked shut, it made him spring up out of bed.

It was his hotel room, he could see that. Somebody had just left. Was it housekeeping, peeking in to see if the room was clear to clean then making a hasty retreat? He looked at the flashing clock on the TV. It was a couple of minutes past six o'clock. Housekeeping would not be in until after eight at the earliest. Who'd been in his room?

He leant across the covers to switch on the lamp. There was a pink bra on the crumpled sheet at the end of the bed. Matt's mind became sharp. What had happened last night?

He looked at the bra. It was Agent Provocateur, very classy and expensive. Matt threw it to the side of the room. What had he done? He remembered walking up the stairs with Victoria. They were laughing at something or other, and he felt drunk and extremely light-headed. But, much as he'd enjoyed Victoria's company, he didn't fancy her. He'd gone through that thought process earlier in the evening.

Is she attractive? Yes!
Do I fancy her? No!
Why don't I fancy her? She's nice – but she's not Clare.
Would I consider it? No – I love Clare.

So why was this bra in his bed? And why had somebody – presumably Victoria – just crept out of his room? What did they call it? The walk of shame?

Matt rubbed his eyes and sighed. Had they slept together? He flicked over the sheets looking for telltale signs. To his horror he found the foil wrapper of a condom. He didn't even carry the things, he didn't need them. Clare was on the pill. They'd used them for about a month as teenagers, but had too many scares, and Clare had opted for the pharmaceutical solution before she had turned nineteen. Victoria must have brought it with her.

Matt hunted frantically for the condom, but found nothing. Had she flushed it? He jumped out of bed and ran his hand through the bin. He wasn't sure what he was searching for. Perhaps they'd wrapped it in a tissue and thrown it away. Nothing. He examined himself, checking for signs of dried semen on his skin. Maybe, maybe not. He might have been imagining it.

Jesus, had he cheated on Clare? He'd never been unfaithful to her, never even seriously considered it. Of course, he'd looked at other women and sometimes wondered if they'd thrown their lot in too early. But he loved her, and when you fall in love so young you have to stick with it and see where it goes. So far, it had gone pretty well.

Who else knew? Who had seen him and Victoria together? If only he could remember. He simply couldn't recall what had happened.

Matt didn't even consider telling Clare. It was as hackneyed as excuses come, but he couldn't remember doing anything so it really had meant nothing. There would be no repeats or re-runs, it was never happening again and should never have happened in the first place. Thank God there was evidence of a condom, so he wouldn't need to get himself tested or put Clare off sex until he'd had himself checked over for rashes, diseases or any of the other delights that can accompany unprotected sex.

He'd have to carry the secret and the guilt. There could be no telling. He hated himself for planning to keep it to himself, but if Clare ever found out, the trust would be severed between them. It would be hard to recover from that.

Matt had no appetite for going back to sleep. He straightened out the sheets and picked up his clothes. They were thrown all over the place. That was strange. Clare always teased him about how he folded his clothes into a neat pile at night.

He was ready for the hotel breakfast the minute they started serving. His head was pounding and he drank several coffees to help him come round before tucking into the fried breakfast. He was first up. There was no sign of Victoria or anybody else from the night before. His stomach was settled, it was his head that was causing the problems. Whichever way he ran through the evening, Matt felt certain he hadn't drunk that much. He'd stopped drinking the moment he'd realised that he'd had too much on the train. He was as sure as he could be that he hadn't been pissed.

Thoughts about what he'd done preyed on his mind all weekend. He answered endless questions, made his presentations, chatted with the other contenders. There was no sign of Victoria. If he could only ask her what had happened. The best he could get was: *Probably dealing with some business for Sebastian.* She was supposed to be part of the selection process, it was on the programme, but she was nowhere to be seen. Perhaps she too felt the shame of it.

The success of the weekend was completely obscured by the weight of disappointment in himself for cheating on Clare. Matt was disgusted at what he'd done.

He spent the return journey trying to watch a film on Netflix. He'd begin to watch, get distracted by thoughts of Friday night, and then have to start all over again.

As the train passed York and began to near Newcastle, Matt wondered if Clare would be able to tell. She knew him so well; could he hide something as serious as a betrayal? What about the first time they had sex afterwards – would he give himself away? He doubted if he was capable of deceit. He didn't know if he was up for it. He had no appetite for living a life haunted by lies, he wanted to be honest with Clare. But the thought of her leaving him? It was too much to bear.

As he got out of the taxi, he hesitated outside the front

door. The price of his ambition had already been high: long hours, financial pressures and tense debates about the future. Could the relationship take a revelation like this? He sighed and drew out his front door key, still not knowing what he was going to say to Clare.

CHAPTER SEVENTEEN

October, Helix Fort

Sebastian was nowhere to be seen. In fact, several people were conspicuous by their absence. Olaf had decided not to put in an appearance and Victoria had disappeared without a trace. Eddy had emerged from his crafty cigarette up on the lighthouse, but only to ensure that everything was keeping to time.

Matt was hungry. They were sitting down to eat at eight-thirty, and that was later than he liked to have his evening meal. He swiped a handful of peanuts from the bar and threw them into his mouth. Clare saw what he was doing and give him a look.

It turned out that Phyllis and Vinden were hosting the tour. It made sense, since they'd done the refit. Gina and David had seen it already, but had brought the dogs along anyway. They said it would substitute for their evening walk and help keep the fat off. Matt wasn't sure if they were still referring to the dogs. Jerry was there, a little sozzled, but perfectly capable of making sensible and coherent conversation. He seemed grateful for the company. Quentin and Hunter were eager to get a proper look at the place. It was a makeover dream come true for them. Kylie joined them

too, glamorous in a sequined red mini-dress with her blonde hair artfully tousled.

Matt couldn't stop worrying about what was going on elsewhere. Were Olaf and Sebastian forging a great deal in that conference room? Had he made the wrong call earlier?

'We'll continue with the weekend as planned,' Sebastian had told him. 'I won't make the announcement until late on Sunday.'

He still needed to pick his moment to tell Clare what they'd agreed. He daren't drop that information on her before the meal. It would be better to wait until morning.

'Let's make a start then, shall we?'

When Vinden addressed the group he sounded authoritative but also pompous. Matt hadn't picked that up earlier. The couple were obviously proud of their construction project – and rightly so – but they weren't particularly gracious about it. As they shared information about the purchase and refurbishment, they spared no details about how this was their brainchild and that Sebastian Helix had only pumped in the money and taken delivery of a show home.

'That dog just took a shit on the carpet, did you see?' Jerry sidled up to Matt. 'Wonder which poor bugger is going to clear that up?'

Matt almost burst out laughing. He could see that Gina and David were ignoring the offending item. Some poor soul would cop for that job after they'd left on the Sunday afternoon, probably a minimum wage cleaner from

Portsmouth, expecting to clean up after human beings and discovering that the small print had neglected to mention pampered dogs.

Despite his dislike for their self-importance, Matt found the couple's tour fascinating, particularly when they went behind closed doors into areas which were marked as Staff Only. The renovated fort was an astonishing feat. It was incredible that the technology had existed to build the original in the nineteenth century, and it was equally astonishing to see what it had become with an injection of three million pounds of cash and the undoubted skills of Phyllis and Vinden.

The upper levels were impressive enough: ten luxury bedrooms, beautifully furnished, each with an opulent bathroom; four function rooms, including the mess hall where they'd be dining later that evening; two bars; a games room, and conference room facilities. And of course there was the lighthouse and the deck that looked like a landscaped garden with hot tubs, sauna, patio burners, fire pit and yoga area.

It was when they moved down the staircase to the lower level that the place became even more intriguing. They stepped out into an open area situated below the main deck.

'The entire fort is powered by these two generators,' Phyllis had shouted over the drone of the huge machines. 'There's no power or drainage from the mainland. It's all provided on the structure itself.'

'What happens if they fail?' Hunter asked, genuinely inquisitive. The newbies to the fort were hanging on every word, however pretentiously it was delivered.

'There's a back-up,' Vinden replied. 'It's highly unlikely that both would fail, but if they did, it would be very dark out here.'

There was polite laughter. It didn't bear thinking about.

'The backup supply would power emergency lighting, enough to allow people to move about safely, boats to dock and helicopters to land or take-off.'

'How about phones and broadband?' Matt asked, ever the tech-head.

'Broadband is via satellite and phone signals can sometimes find a mast on the shore, but as you've probably discovered, when the weather gets bad it can become a little erratic. We use traditional radio comms for emergency use, of course. So, whatever happens, we're pretty well covered.'

They moved on to the empty control room and then the cellars, which were packed with what looked like very expensive wines. Matt and Clare didn't really know. They were a Blue-Nun-from-the-local-supermarket kind of couple. Matt suspected that these wines weren't generally consumed on a faded settee in front of the TV accompanied by a bowl of cheesy something-or-others.

As the rest of the group began admiring the vintages of the bottles in the racks, Kylie sidled up to him.

'Incredible, isn't it?'

'It certainly is. I can't believe how vast it is.'

'What did Sebastian say to you in there? Anything interesting?'

She was watching Clare, who was chatting to Quentin and Hunter. She was making sure they wouldn't be disturbed.

'My guess is that he made you an offer, right? He wants to buy you out.'

Matt's face was burning. He looked away, pretending to be interested in the wines.

'Look, this is a Château Lafite-Rothschild 2009. That can't be very valuable. It's only a few years old.'

'It's worth over seven thousand pounds, so don't drop it. And you evaded my question.'

'Jesus!' Matt said, placing the bottle back in its rack. The stakes weren't quite so high when holding a bottle of Blue Nun.

'I'm not at liberty to discuss what happened—'

'You sound like a copper on the TV!' Kylie snapped at him. 'Come on, what did he say? I'll bet he offered to buy you out at a rock bottom price. Tell me I'm wrong.'

Matt wondered if he'd been an idiot.

'I haven't even discussed it with Clare yet. I'm not going to say,' he replied.

The group began to move out of the cellar and along the white-painted, curving brick corridor of the lower level. Matt was grateful to be separated from Kylie as they went.

Vinden suddenly swung round to face them, brandishing a black automatic rifle.

'Stop where you are!'

There was a momentary gasp of shock and then more polite laughter.

'Paintball or laser battles!' he chuckled. 'Sometimes Sebastian hires out the fort for corporate events. The network of rooms and tunnels down here makes for a marvellous game of hide-and-seek.'

It was the perfect location for it, a labyrinth of rooms and passageways to hunt and be hunted.

'There are some more rooms on the far side for the paintball battles,' said Phyllis, holding up another of the rifles alongside a facemask. 'You certainly wouldn't want to fire one of these against Sebastian's white walls.'

Matt apologised as his stomach rumbled loudly.

'I think it's about that time,' said Vinden, leading them back towards the staircase. 'If you thought all of this was impressive, wait until you see what they can rustle up in the kitchens. You're in for a treat tonight.'

As they began to file up the stairs, Matt was aware of Kylie manoeuvring her way over to him. Ever the journalist, she was coming to get her question answered. They were last on the staircase, and he was trapped.

'Come on. What was it? Did he make you a ridiculously low offer or did he tell you he's giving it to Olaf? I promise I won't tell.'

'I'm not saying anything until I've spoken to Clare. Why do you care, anyway? It makes no difference to you, you're not part of the competition.'

'We all need to care about what's going on in Sebastian Helix's life. There's something not right here.'

'Oh? Has he told you something? You're here for a book deal, aren't you?'

'That's right. There's never been an authorised biography of him before.'

'And?' Matt pushed. 'So what's the big deal?'

'I expected to walk away with a cash offer to write it,' Kylie continued, holding onto the rail to avoid slipping on the steps, 'but instead he's offering a share of royalties and only a tiny fee upfront.'

'So what?' Matt asked, none the wiser.

'A man like Sebastian Helix? A sure-fire hit like this? I expected to walk out of here with a six-figure offer to ghost-write it for him. It's normal to pay someone like me a fee upfront. He admitted that he can't manage that at the moment. He's got cash-flow problems, Matt. I reckon he's fighting for survival!'

CHAPTER EIGHTEEN

October, Helix Fort

'Welcome everybody!' said Sebastian as he walked into the bar area and all heads turned. Victoria Winterton was with him. She looked stunning in a black dress and heels. She was wearing a shawl around her shoulders and a light but clearly expensive necklace. Gina and Phyllis dripped wealth, but on Victoria it sat subtly, a complement to her natural demeanour. She wore it well.

There was still no sign of Olaf. In fact, all the guests were there apart from him. That was fast becoming the norm. If they'd wheeled in a big cake and Olaf had burst out of it wearing a mankini, Matt wouldn't have been surprised. He had to make it through until Sunday without killing the man.

Eddy was conspicuous by his absence too. But then he didn't seem to be part of the proceedings. His role appeared to be as a facilitator.

'Help yourself to drinks, everybody. We'll move into the mess hall in five minutes.'

The chatter picked up once again and Sebastian made his way over to Matt and Clare.

'You look absolutely stunning, Clare,' he said, making her blush. She could tell he meant it and it made her feel more at ease among the other guests. Sebastian was almost a mirror image of Matt: smart trousers, open-neck shirt and a jacket. Nothing showy, not too scruffy. He breathed a sigh of relief. If the top man wasn't in a lounge suit or dinner jacket, he'd made the right choice. Clare gave him a small smile.

'I wanted to thank you for your time earlier, Matt. Remember what we discussed about confidentiality. I wanted to catch you before you-know-who arrives and to remind you to ignore anything he says to you. Carry on as we agreed.'

As if on cue, Olaf walked into the room. This time there was no fuss, no big entrance. And he was dressed appropriately too, even a little more formally than Matt. He steered clear of the other guests and ordered a drink at the bar, staying there for a few minutes and chatting to the barman.

Matt thought that he looked unusually tense.

'I guess the stress must even get to Olaf Strauss sometimes!'

Sebastian smiled. 'In the interests of fair play, I should give him the same pep talk as you. Remember to enjoy your evening. I want you to savour the whole experience this weekend. Have confidence – you've come this far!'

He headed over towards Olaf. Matt turned to Clare.

'I told you an open-neck shirt would be fine. You can't go far wrong if you follow the man in charge.'

'Okay, okay, I admit it. You were right. Look, here's

Kylie. Do you mind if I go and chat to her? Jerry looks like he could do with a pal over there.'

Matt nodded and Clare headed over to Kylie, who'd already spotted her and was making a beeline for her new friend. The women were completely at ease with each other. Matt figured that the evening would go more smoothly if Clare got to sit with her friend. It would free him to work the room and glean whatever tips and advice he could.

'Have you seen Victoria bloody Winterton? Do you think she knew I'd be wearing black tonight? It's like she wanted to piss me off ...'

Matt caught the beginning of his wife's conversation and decided to take her hint and join Jerry. He was nursing a glass of wine at the bar. Although he'd showered and dressed carefully for the evening, Matt could tell that he'd been drinking heavily.

'You alright, Jerry? You look like you've got something on your mind.'

Jerry looked up, pleased to see him. His words were slightly slurred.

'Bloody ex-wife emailed me. She wants a share of any future royalties now. I may as well chop off both bollocks and send them to her in the mail. She says that if she's raising the children, they have a right to be able to enjoy a share of my future income. She's got good lawyers too, paid for by me. It's a mess, Matt. Don't ever get divorced from that lovely wife of yours. Hang onto her for dear life.'

Matt looked over towards Clare. She was laughing with Kylie, her face lit up. He loved seeing it. They'd been stuck in the same furrow for months – maybe this weekend would be just what they needed.

'Best go easy on the drink,' he suggested, knowing he was on dodgy ground.

'You sound like my wife!' Jerry replied, prepared to be angry. But he checked himself. 'It's my fault. I do need to lay off the drink. It's hard when you've been part of something for so long and then it ends. The band's been my life. I miss the guys.'

It was a surreal moment. Matt could never have imagined that he'd find himself giving advice to the man whose CDs had been at the centre of his music collection.

'Do you think you'll make up?'

'The band or the marriage?'

'I was thinking of the band.'

'No, that won't happen. There's no way Pat wants to go on the road again. He wrote the songs and makes the most money. He's loaded and will remain so until the day he dies and some time afterwards. I don't get the same royalties. And I can't make it as a solo artist, my songs aren't strong enough – Sebastian must know that. I'm feeling shafted, truth be told. This might be it. I have a right hand that's insured for a million pounds, but I can't make any money from it unless I end up in my own pub tribute act.'

'A million pounds! That's incredible.'

'It's not incredible, it's sad. If I don't pull something off quickly, there's no way I'll get that level of insurance when it comes up for renewal. It'll be worth no more than a ten-year-old Ford Fiesta.'

'Look, I really don't want to sound like your wife, but you'll stand a much better chance of landing a deal with Sebastian if you're sober. Whatever it is he offers you, you can start rebuilding your life from there.'

'You're a good guy,' Jerry said sincerely. 'I hope Seb picks you, you deserve it. That little git over there ...' he nodded at Olaf, who had already moved on from Sebastian and joined Clare and Kylie, '... I've seen his kind in the music industry. They'd eat their own young if they were peckish. Seb should be careful.'

A gong sounded and Sebastian ushered them through the double doors that had opened to the side of the bar into the mess hall. In front of them was a long table of polished oak, each place set with silver cutlery and crystal glasses sparkling in the light of the candles positioned around the room. Classical music was playing gently in the background. Ready to greet them were three waiting staff dressed smartly in black waistcoats and bow ties. Matt thought it worked superbly.

There were no places allocated and they walked into the room unsure who would sit where. Matt tried to move towards Clare, but found himself cut off at the end of the table. He looked around. It was the seating plan from hell. He was sitting opposite Kylie, who'd been separated from Clare by Olaf. Olaf had a woman on either side of him. That was no accident.

Matt had the only spare seat next to him and he'd just seen who would be taking that place. It was Victoria Winterton, who'd stayed behind in the bar and was the last to join the group. As she sat next to him, almost directly opposite Clare, Matt gave his wife a look to convey that it had been a random misfortune.

There were menus at the table. Matt hadn't anticipated he'd have to read anything.

'Excuse me, I won't be long. I didn't bring my glasses,' he said to Victoria.

He stood up and walked around the table to Clare.

'I've got to get my glasses,' he said. 'Won't be a moment.'

Then, quietly, in her ear, 'I'm sorry about the seating, it was an accident.'

'I know. It can't be helped. Go and get your glasses, it's always best if you have them with you.'

Matt slipped out, largely unnoticed. All activity was now focused on the mess hall. The rest of the fort was quiet, except for the sound of dogs barking as he walked along the curving corridor past what must have been Gina and David's suite.

He made his way to his room and quickly retrieved his glasses. He couldn't resist taking a few minutes to check the pen drive. It was still there, he could relax. Then, with glasses in his jacket pocket, he headed back to the bar area.

Something wasn't right. The hubbub of chatter that he'd left was now silent. An unfamiliar male voice appeared to be addressing them all. He was speaking with a French accent – it wasn't one of the guests.

He slowed before he entered the double doors. The barman was no longer there. Matt could feel the tension and he wasn't even back inside. Cautiously he peered around the door. He'd been right to hold back. Three men were stationed around the room, the guests still seated. The waiting staff and the chef were on their knees facing the far wall, with a fourth man watching over them with a hand-gun. The ringleader – who was addressing the terrified dinner guests – was pointing a gun at Sebastian Helix's head, his finger precariously placed on the trigger.

CHAPTER NINETEEN

September, London, UK

Matt noticed things weren't right as soon as he opened the door. Clare's small suitcase had been abandoned at the bottom of the stairs. There was mud all over the entrance hall and a crumpled newspaper in the living room. She was fussy about things like that; she hated it when the house looked a mess the minute you walked into it. She disliked shoes on carpets too.

He didn't get his normal welcome. She was doing something upstairs. He could hear thumping.

'Hello!' he shouted. 'I'm back!'

The thumping stopped.

'Clare! What's been going on?'

She walked down the stairs. She'd been crying.

'We've been broken into. I found it like this when I got back this morning. Bastards ...'

As her foot landed on the last step, she lunged forward and threw her arms around him.

'God, I'm pleased you're back.'

For a second, Matt wondered if she could sense his tension. Would she be able to smell the deceit on him?

'Why didn't you ring me?' he asked as she drew away from him.

'And mess up your big weekend? It wouldn't have changed anything. I decided to deal with it on my own.'

'Whose are the footprints?'

'Cops. They don't train them to wipe their feet apparently.'

'Did anything get stolen?'

'They've not taken anything as far as I can see – not that we've got much to take. But they've had a good rummage around looking for something or other, and they were very interested in our tech. Everything had been left switched on.'

'Did the cops get any fingerprints? Any clues?'

'Nothing. Whoever it was knew what they were doing. No prints. They didn't even damage the doors. They appear to have walked straight in and straight out again. The police have logged it, but they don't think anything will come of it. We can't even claim on insurance. The cops did more damage with their muddy boots.'

'Just give me a minute,' Matt said touching her on the side of her hip and preparing to run up the stairs.

'Shoes!' Clare chided him. He was going to suggest that it was a bit late, but thought better of it. Off came the shoes and he headed up to his office. He felt around for the pen drive taped to the back of the bookcase. It was still there. He'd got extra verification on his cloud account, and he'd received no alerts over the weekend. If that's what they were looking for, they hadn't found it.

'All fine?' Clare asked when he came downstairs. She'd

got the kettle on. He loved being home. He loved the feeling of it. How could he have ended up in bed with Victoria ... what was he thinking?

'I agree with you, there's nothing missing. Nothing broken either. I thought for a minute they might have been after my files. There's been enough publicity about it in the papers. Some idiot might have decided to try his luck at stealing my idea.'

'But if they were amateurs, they'd have broken the locks, wouldn't they? Whoever was in the house knew what they were doing. That's what the coppers said.'

'Well, they left empty-handed. Even if they'd got the pen drive, they wouldn't have got the second part of the files. They're in my cloud account, encrypted and locked down.'

'How was your weekend?' Clare asked, handing him a cup of tea.

He didn't really want to discuss it.

'I'm through to the final selection.'

'Oh, brilliant!' She put down her tea to hug him. 'Well done! What was the competition like?'

'Tricky, but they must have liked my pitch. It's me and some other guy. He's a bit of a prick but has an amazing concept. And you won't believe where we get to go next ... and this time you can join me.'

The evening was taken up with the inevitable note exchanges. Clare's wedding had been fun, the weekend travel had been its usual trial on public transport and she'd had a wonderful couple of days until she walked into the house and saw what had happened.

Matt glossed over all the social elements of his adventures, focusing instead on the time spent making pitches and having his ideas scrutinised. When Clare suggested an early night he made his excuses and went straight to sleep. He wasn't ready to risk intimacy so early into his deception – he still needed to think things through.

He was doing just that the next day when he and Clare bumped into each other on the high street. He'd gone to check with his insurance broker if they could claim to change the locks. Clare had walked into town with him and left him, supposedly to go to the post office. He walked directly into her as she exited the jobcentre. If she'd managed not to look quite so guilty, he wouldn't have challenged her, assuming she was seeing what other jobs might be available.

'Hello, you!' he said, then seeing the look on her face, 'What were you up to in there?'

Clare looked at him, and then decided to come clean.

'It's probably an appropriate time to tell you, now you're in the final of the competition. I've lost my job. Franco is closing the restaurant. He's going to work with his brother.'

'Shit!' was Matt's response. He swiftly worked through that month's bills in his head, adding in the excess he'd have to pay if he wanted the locks changed. They'd have to stay as they were.

'That's not good. When did you find out?'

Clare decided to lie about that.

'At the end of last week. I didn't want to spook you before your big day.'

'Probably just as well. If I don't get this funding, we're going to have to make some changes. It's going to be touch and go as to whether we make it through this month. I might be joining you in the jobcentre soon.'

Clare was relieved at how well he'd taken it, but was far too embarrassed to admit that she'd been visiting the jobcentre for the past couple of weeks, always deceiving him about where she was going when she left the house.

They walked towards home together, both mulling over the consequences of her joblessness.

'Oh heck, I forgot to pay in my expenses cheque from the weekend. They handed them out while we were in London. Do you want to go ahead and get the kettle on? I'll be back asap.'

They separated and headed off in their different directions. As he neared the bank, he thought about Victoria and what, if anything, he could say to Clare.

Was now the best time for him to come clean? After all, she'd deceived him about losing her job. And it would get harder and harder the longer he left it. He'd have to tell her straightaway or it was a deception that he'd have to carry with him forever.

He waited in the queue at the bank cursing Sebastian Helix for not using direct cash transfer. Cheques were for cavemen and the over-nineties as far as Matt was concerned. Still, it was a good amount – he'd need it to clear as soon as possible. It seemed a strange way for a tech giant to operate.

Matt worried the issue all the way home. Now was the time to strike while Clare was being apologetic. There was no way the two issues would balance out, but it was the best time to admit what had happened. He paused on the doorstep, inserted his key and opened the door. He was going to tell her. Come what may, he knew it was the right thing to do.

He needn't have wasted time worrying about it, because the truth was already out. Instead of Clare's usual cheery welcome, she said nothing when he walked into the living room. She'd been crying and her tablet had been thrown across the room.

'Pick it up!' she screamed at him. 'Pick it up and take a good look at it. You bastard! You said this was all for us and our future. Well, to hell with you!'

She was out of control. Matt thought she was going to leap at him. He'd never seen her this way. He moved over towards the tablet and picked it up, already fearing what he might see.

'You arsehole,' Clare wept. 'You stupid, bloody idiot.'

Matt turned around the tablet and reactivated the screen, which had gone into sleep mode. It was an email with an image attached. There was no longer any doubting what had happened that first night in London. The picture showed Matt naked in bed with Victoria, also wearing no clothes, clearly nuzzled into him on the bed. Her pink bra was lying beside them, almost in the same position that he'd found it. He could also see the condom foil that he'd found tucked into the sheets.

So, Clare knew what had gone on that night. And now, so did he.

PART 2

CHAPTER TWENTY

October, Helix Fort

The moment Matt watched Jerry's finger drop to the floor he understood the seriousness of what was going on. It was a rapid gear change from fifth to reverse. One moment he was bang in the middle of a lavish social event, the next he'd walked onto the set of the Captain Phillips movie. But they were a mile from Portsmouth. This wasn't Somalia.

He paused to watch Clare's face. She was terrified, her eyes darting around trying to make sense of what was happening. She'd spotted him hiding behind the door, but he could see that she was trying to avoid looking in his direction. She was desperate not to give him away.

When the guy in charge ran his hands across her body, lingering around her breasts and squeezing her behind, Matt had to stop himself calling out and bursting into the room in some ridiculous display of macho chivalry. What could he do? They had guns and the kitchen chopper that was supposed to have been used to prepare the steaks had just lopped off the index finger of one of the best guitarists in rock history.

Matt paused a moment before making his retreat. Where was Eddy? Nowhere to be seen. If he could find him, they might be able to figure out this mess together. He took one last look at Clare. They were pushing her to find out where he was. It took all his willpower to pull himself away. He had to raise the alarm.

He whispered the words, *I love you, Clare* to himself. He did love her, there was no doubt about that. All the nonsense in their relationship, the Global Entrepreneur Challenge, Sebastian Helix and his money – none of it mattered. He loved Clare and he was going to get her out of there.

He turned and started to walk back through the bar. He'd thought himself smart picking up the knife that the dead barman had been using, but he realised that he needed a better weapon. On one of the far tables were three bottles of champagne and, of all things, a sabre resting along the seats. They were going to use sabrage to slice off each bottle's neck. It must have been one of the spectacles that Sebastian had in store for them.

Matt ran a quick history lesson in his head. The fort was Napoleonic, and sabrage was one of Napoleon's tricks. He remembered that much from history classes. He also remembered that he'd spent most of the lessons admiring the delightful curves of Clare's blossoming breasts. They were teenagers, intoxicated by their recent discovery of hurried sex at their parents' houses.

He picked up the sabre, hoping it wasn't just for show. He'd only have a minute or two before they sent someone after him, and they'd be armed too. His only advantage was that of surprise. He'd never hit a man in his life. When it came to violence, he didn't know where to start.

He made his way along the curving corridor to the bedrooms. David and Gina's dogs were still barking. He tried their door – it was open. The irony wasn't lost on him. They'd felt no need to lock up since they were among friends. Rich friends. And perhaps they figured that the mutts would defend any valuables in there.

He could hear footsteps behind him. They were coming already. Damn them, he'd barely had time to think. Instinctively he opened the door to David and Gina's bedroom. The dogs rushed towards him, yapping away, but friendly enough. He grabbed a chewy toy that had been discarded on the floor and threw it along the corridor. All three animals ran after it, thinking it was playtime.

Matt ran over to his own room to leave the door ajar, and then concealed himself in David and Gina's room to wait. He heard cursing as the dogs ran into whoever it was that was coming for him. The animals must have sensed that they were up to no good. There was angry barking now, more cursing and then a gunshot. Two more shots. Jesus, had they shot the dogs? Gina and David would never forgive him. It was silent out there now. He could hear movement in his direction.

There were two of them. One had a gun, the other had brought the blood-stained cleaver. They made straight for Matt and Clare's room. Was it Clare who had told them which one it was? Had they hurt her? The bastards, they'd pay for that. He looked at the sabre. It seemed sharp enough, but perhaps that was only at its end. Would it be any use? It was all he had.

'Check the other rooms!'

There were three more doors between his room and the

one he was hiding in. The others were locked and the guy with the cleaver quickly found out that they couldn't be kicked in. Matt ducked to the side of a wardrobe so that he wouldn't be seen when he entered the room.

The door opened and cleaver man stepped cautiously into the room. Matt's heart was thudding. It sounded so loud – surely he wasn't the only one who could hear it?

The man paused to look around the room, assessing what was going on. Matt closed his eyes, gripped the sabre and ran at him screaming. It was the most useless attack ever, but it frightened the life out of his pursuer. As he saw him raise the cleaver to defend himself, Matt held out the sabre and thrust it into his shoulder. Metal crunched on bone as he drove the blade into his flesh with as much strength as he could muster. The man gasped and dropped the cleaver onto the floor.

Matt could hear movement from outside. The henchman with the gun was coming to help his colleague. Matt drew the sabre out of the wounded man's shoulder and kicked the door shut, flipping the lock. He turned back into the room to face his most immediate problem. Despite the blood and his obvious pain, the thug had already picked up the cleaver and was getting ready to launch himself at Matt. There was a thud at the door, then kicking. He'd have two of them to deal with before long, and the one on the other side of the door could shoot him.

Matt reached out and picked up a lamp, tearing the flex out of the wall. He threw it at his attacker, who brushed it away with the cleaver. Matt could see that he'd misjudged the situation. This guy was much more accustomed to violence than he was. He understood what was happening here. Matt had thought that he'd prod him with a sabre and, somehow – magically – he'd fall to the ground dead. Well, that hadn't happened. It had barely made him pause and now he looked seriously pissed.

'Give it up, arsehole!'

Another French accent.

Still the kicking at the door. Matt had to make his move. He ran at cleaver man again, sabre pointing outwards, a repeat of the manoeuvre that had worked so well for him before. This time his assailant was ready and fended off the blade with a sweep of the cleaver. Matt dropped the sabre and crashed into him.

The kicking at the door was now making an impact. Matt could see the lock loosening from its screws. He didn't have long. Behind him he sensed the cleaver being drawn up ready to strike.

A fist slammed into his stomach. The blow caused him to drop to his knees. He'd never felt anything like it before. His eyes were streaming. He needed a few minutes to recover, but there was no time. He rolled off to the side, just missing the blade of the cleaver as it swung by his head. The bastard had been going for the kill.

If any part of Matt had thought this was a charade, that was now over. He got it. He had to kill this idiot. Ignoring the intense, sickening pain in his stomach, he reached out for the sabre. He grasped its handle and turned to face the assassin who was coming for him again.

He needed to get up onto his feet – he was too vulner-able on the floor – but his stomach hurt so much. The man was rushing at him, cleaver in hand. The lock looked like it might withstand one, maybe two, more kicks. As his attacker leapt at him, Matt thrust out his own weapon, closed his eyes and hoped for the best.

The sabre became heavy in Matt's hand and then crashed to the floor. The cleaver dropped to the side of his head, brushing his cheek. Matt opened his eyes to find himself face to face with the man who'd been trying to kill him. He was impaled on the sword, gradually sliding along its blade. A trickle of blood ran down Matt's hand. He let go of the handle and cleaver man collapsed down to his side.

The door burst open. He barely had time to think. Next to him was the dying man and ahead of him another thug levelling up his gun and getting ready to shoot. Matt reached out for the cleaver and flung it with every last bit of strength. It sank deep into the second man's head.

'And you can get lost too!' he yelled, as his new attacker crashed to the floor, a look of surprise still on his bloody face, his skull now neatly split by a kitchen utensil.

CHAPTER TWENTY-ONE

October, Helix Fort

Matt took a moment to breathe, but threw up instead. He'd never as much as hit anybody in his life before and within the space of a minute he'd killed two men.

He stood up and wiped his face. The man impaled on the sabre was still twitching. Matt hadn't a clue how long it took a man to die from a sword attack. In real life he figured organs would get damaged and death would be slow and painful. In films the baddies died like the second man had – fast and without fuss. He didn't know what to do, but one thing was for sure: that sabre was staying where he'd left it – right through the heart.

Still terrified, he was shaking uncontrollably. He thanked his lucky stars that he'd hit a vital organ. And he had a weapon now, a gun. He didn't know how to use it, but it was better than a cleaver or a sabre. It would be more threatening – he'd only have to wave it around to get some attention.

The gun was heavier than he'd expected. It felt good to have it in his hand, he felt more powerful. His stomach was cramping, but he knew he'd have to move on. He needed to get out of there.

He didn't know how many there were in the gang. He'd seen three in the dining room. He'd killed two of them, but were there more? He couldn't even be sure that these two men had been in the mess hall. How many thugs did it take to overcome a sea fort?

Matt looked at the men he'd killed. The man who'd had the gun was covered in tattoos, the sort that you used to see on guys who'd been in the armed forces. There was a scorpion in there and a skull and crossbones. Nothing artistic like the millennials preferred.

He was big bugger. Matt was pleased that he hadn't had to use the sabre on him. Sabre guy was still now, he'd stopped his twitching. Matt couldn't believe what he'd just done.

He stepped out of the room, trying to remember where the control rooms had been during the earlier tour. The fort wasn't massive. It had held a couple of hundred soldiers in its day and now, in more luxurious times, could accommodate maybe twenty or so guests and whatever staff were needed to look after them. However, the curving corridors could be disorientating and he struggled to remember the location of the staircase where Kylie had tried to nobble him about his conversation with Sebastian.

It could only have been an hour ago, less probably. How had things turned to shit so fast? Matt couldn't get his head around it. What was their plan? They must be there for the cash. Were they going to ransom the guests? They were all worth a few bob, except for him and Clare, and the staff. They were expendable. Once they realised what he'd done, they'd come for him. He had to stay ahead of them. He had to take care of Clare. She was his priority.

Matt found the doorway to the staircase and made his way down towards the control room. Gina and David had explained earlier how it was barely used by Sebastian. There was CCTV across the fort, but it was used mainly at night when all the guests were tucked up in bed. They'd chuckled as they commented that you don't get a lot of break-ins from sea creatures when you're out at sea.

He quickly found the office area. It looked as if it had been built into the design, but it was bigger than needed. It had all the fittings you would expect to find in a more commercial operation. Other forts in the Solent ran as commercial ventures. Perhaps this had been one of them before Sebastian Helix bought it as his millionaire's man cave.

Matt noticed the CCTV was switched on. If he could get a look at the screens, it might give him an idea of what he was dealing with. There was sure to be some kind of communication console there too. They must have some ship-to-shore arrangement. He hadn't a clue how things worked at sea.

There were twenty monitors, only two of them switched on, giving Matt a clear view of the helipad and the docking area. That made sense. Perhaps it was Eddy's job to keep an eye on arrivals and departures. Matt pressed the buttons on the other monitors and one-by-one they fired up.

He examined the first two screens. On the one showing the docking area he could see two armed men. So, there must have been as many as six of them in the gang. He'd killed two, but that still left four of them on the fort, but only if he'd counted them correctly. They all looked the same to Matt. Big, brawny and violent. The view on the second screen was the most disturbing. All three of the catering staff plus the chef had been herded into the middle of the helipad and were kneeling down. They'd been taken as they were in their thin indoor clothing and were now exposed to the extremities with no windbreaks or walls to shelter behind. Matt couldn't see any of the guests. He supposed Helix's staff would be considered lower value captives. The cash cows were still in the dining area.

Matt thought he heard a sound from the corridor beyond the office. He paused and listened. It was nothing, he'd been mistaken.

The other screens were now displaying images from around the fort. Most of them were bland shots of corridors or stairwells, but a couple of the screens gave him the information that he was after.

He had two views of the dining room. All the guests had been seated at the table and were still sitting there. A man was circling them, waving a shotgun around dangerously. There was no sound. Matt could only imagine the threats that were being levelled at them.

Jerry was nowhere to be seen. Was he dead? Matt had no idea if he could have survived the amputation. He ran through his limited knowledge of arteries and bleeding and was still none the wiser.

Something caught Matt's eye on one of the other monitors. It was only there for a moment. It was one of the dogs. It seemed a ridiculous victory, given what was playing out, but Matt was relieved that at least one of David and Gina's pets had survived.

Then, more movement from another camera. He could see Eddy walking along a corridor, but Matt had no idea where. He was holding a gun. How had Eddy got a gun? Matt supposed it made sense. Somebody like Sebastian

Helix had to have protection and perhaps that was Eddy's role. Maybe he was ex-military. Did Eddy know about his escape from the dining room? Matt needed to find him. Between the two of them they might be able to organise some kind of rescue.

He scanned the area for communications devices. He'd left his own phone in his room, and in any case there was no signal. To the side of the screens was a radio set. He played with the buttons but couldn't figure out how to use it.

Two of the men from the boat were moving up the steps towards the upper level of the fort. Something was happening. Then, frightening in its volume, an announcement suddenly boomed out over the public address system. Matt didn't recognise the voice, but he clocked the French accent.

'Mr Dalton, we know you're hiding on the fort. We require your presence in the mess hall. You can't have failed to notice that there's no way on or off this structure that doesn't go through us. You're stuck. Either you make yourself known to us or we'll flush you out. If we have to flush you out, we're going to start killing people. It's up to you, Mr Dalton.'

Matt saw that there was a microphone in the office. For a moment he was tempted to speak, to tell them to piss off, but he thought better of it. Clare was up there. He could see her on the CCTV, not clear enough to make out her face, but she had to be terrified. Matt was certainly scared out of his wits, but he knew he had to start picking them off. The adrenalin was driving him on. He had to join Eddy. But first he needed to find a toilet.

CHAPTER TWENTY-TWO

October, Helix Fort

As far as Matt could tell, they had no way of tracking where he was on the fort. He needed to stay undetected and figure out how he could get a message to the world outside. He ran through his choices. The tech was the obvious way. If he could get to his devices, he'd be able to raise the alarm. But they weren't stupid, they'd know he would want to head back to his room.

He messed around with the radio dials again. Every now and then he'd catch part of a conversation, but he hadn't a clue what you had to do to raise a human being. Where was Eddy? He'd know how to operate all this stuff.

Matt watched the screens. He reckoned there were perhaps six more of them.

Six more men to beat, two dead already. At least he and Eddy both had a gun. He decided to smash the screens. If they figured out that they could monitor the entire fort, they'd find him in no time. He looked for something to break the glass. All he needed now was a lacerated hand. He thought about Jerry again. As he scoured the room, he found a container of safety flares. He stuffed three of them into his back pocket. He'd seen the movies. There are a lot of things you can do with a safety flare.

He settled on destroying the screens with a fire extinguisher. He had a quick look along the corridor before he started to make sure he was alone. But he could see them all anyway – on the helipad, by the boat and in the mess hall, all of them accounted for. He smashed those three screens last. He hoped he wasn't cutting off his nose to spite his face.

Would he have time to grab his tech from his room? He'd have to be fast. As soon as the final screens were broken, he picked up the gun and headed for the stairs, all the time listening. He made his way silently along the curved corridor. He was nearing Gina and David's room. He glanced inside. The bodies had been rolled over, the sabre and cleaver removed, but otherwise they'd been left where he killed them.

There was a noise to his right, a whimpering sound coming from along the corridor. It was one of the dogs. It had been shot. Matt considered the wisdom in risking his life to save a dog. It was madness. But it felt like any victory, however small, was worth fighting for.

He made his way up the corridor. There was a lot of blood. It had been hit twice, one a graze, the other wound more serious. Matt wasn't particularly an animals kind of guy, but he comforted the creature and lifted it gently from the floor. The best place to take it seemed to be David and Gina's room, despite the two dead bodies lying on the floor. The dogs had a basket there, toys and water, so at least it would be comfortable if it didn't make it.

Matt found a first aid kit in the bathroom tucked into one of the units. He bandaged the wounds as best he could, snipping away the dog's hair and putting a plaster on the graze. The dog was called Scooby, it had a tag. Matt instantly loved the name. It reminded him of a childhood spent watching cartoons.

'You'll be okay, just sit tight,' he said, stroking Scooby's fur. He made sure that his new friend was as comfortable as possible, moved the water bowl next to the dog bed, and then checked the corridor again. It was clear. He decided to risk a dash to his bedroom to check his phone and tech.

The room had been ransacked. Clothes were strewn over the bed and the few belongings that they'd carried with them thrown onto the floor. Their phones had been stamped on and his laptop was gone. Matt rushed to the mattress where he'd hidden the pen drive – it was still there, they hadn't found it.

He picked up the phones, checking them to see if he could squeeze some life from them. Both were wrecked. He slipped out their SIM cards, wrapping them in a small piece of notepaper so that they wouldn't fall out of his pocket. They were so goddamn small.

Once again the public address system sprang into life. It was quieter this time, and he had to walk into the corridor to hear it.

'Mr Dalton, or should I call you Matt? That's what your beautiful wife calls you. And by the way she's hot, very hot. If you'd care to move to where you can get a look at the helipad you'll see your lovely wife getting ready for a swim. Soon she's going to be very wet. If you don't get your arse up here by the count of twenty, she goes into the sea.'

'Fuck!' Matt shouted, touching the flares in his back pocket and checking the gun.

He ran out into the corridor, now with no fears for his safety. He was pointing his gun. If he saw any of the bastards he'd shoot straight through them. He ran out onto the deck, bypassing the bar, and sped towards the metal steps of the landing pad.

He paused on the lower step, not knowing what was going to greet him. Gun extended, he walked slowly to the top of the steps. The helipad was surrounded by safety lights and bathed in brightness by a spotlight. There were two men there, both armed. Matt had heard one of them was called Alby, he was an ugly brute with curly hair that looked like it needed a good wash. He was waving his gun at the chef and three waiting staff who were kneeling with their hands behind their heads. Yves, Sebastian's chef, was sobbing, they were scared for their lives.

By the edge of the platform, her black dress ripped at the side, was Clare. The man called Leon was gripping her arm, bruising it. He held a gun to her head.

Again the voice boomed out from the speaker.

'Three … two … one. Come out, come out wherever you are, Mr Dalton!'

'Matt! Oh God, Matt, you shouldn't have come.'

Clare sounded broken. Leon shook her roughly to shut her up and then looked over towards the lighthouse. He gave a thumbs up. Matt couldn't see who he was looking at but a signal had clearly been passed. Leon lowered his gun and gave Clare another firm shake.

'You stupid fool! You should have stayed put.'

He turned away from Matt and without blinking threw Clare off the side of the helipad.

'Jesus Christ!' Matt yelled.

He levelled up his gun, pointed it directly at Leon and shot him twice through the head. He fell to the ground, a splash of crimson spreading slowly from his shattered skull. There was a gasp from the hostages, and even their captor seemed to be in shock, unsure of how to react.

Matt had no such doubts. He did what any man who loved his wife would do. He dropped his gun and ran towards the edge of the pad as fast as he could. He knew that he had a net to clear. He'd need to jump as wide as possible. He was going in after Clare. And if he couldn't save her, they'd drown together.

CHAPTER TWENTY-THREE

October, Helix Fort

Matt knew he'd made a stupid decision the moment he began his sprint towards the edge of the helipad, but all he could think of was trying to save Clare. The waves were fierce and black, the light very limited, and the prospect of entering the water terrifying. But what else could he have done? In that split second, he'd chosen Clare.

It had hurt falling into the water from that height. He'd not thought to dive but had performed the world's most dangerous water bomb, dropping like a dead weight into the sea's powerful darkness. He immediately began to thrash about, desperate to reach the surface where he could fill his lungs with air.

He knew his chances were poor. His finest achievement as a swimmer was a certificate for swimming 100 metres in a municipal pool. That was it. He'd swum a few times as an adult, but who needs to swim any distance unless they're a lifeguard, an extra in Baywatch, or it's their go-to keep-fit strategy? None of those applied to him. Clare, however, was the proverbial water baby. She'd swum for the school team until she became more interested in her relationship with Matt and teenage infatuation got in the way.

Matt spat out a mouthful of water and tried to steady his breathing. His clothes were immediately wet and heavy, hindering his movements. Messing around in a chlorinated pool in his Speedos was considerably different from battling the crashing waves of the sea fully clothed.

He tried to scan the area, but he was bobbing up and down so much it was almost impossible. The waves appeared to be taking him away from the fort. That wasn't good. He needed to find something to hang onto. He looked up. A couple of iron pathways ran around the circumference of the fort. He'd seen photos in the bar of people fishing from those. They'd give a great vantage point for shooting at him too.

The side of the structure was lined with lights and he was near enough for this to be of some advantage as he struggled to keep afloat. However, he could see the blackness ahead of him. If he didn't work hard to stay within that illuminated area, he'd be carried out to sea and would have little chance of surviving.

There was no sign of Clare. For all he knew, she might be dead already. If she'd struck the railings on the way down, there was no way she'd have survived. Instead of looking for a swimmer, Matt began to search for a body. A strong wave lifted him up high, and then dropped him down in a dip. As he rose up again, a wave hit his face and he missed a breath. He fought for air, but he'd panicked and lost his rhythm. He was expending too much energy and quickly tiring. He turned towards the fort. One of the men was on the metal pathway scouring the water with a flashlight. He was holding a gun. Matt kept as low in the water as he dared, but it was difficult, the waves were a powerful rival.

Then two shots. He'd barely heard them over the sound of the sea, but he'd seen the flash from the weapon. They weren't aimed at him. He looked over to where the gun had been pointing. Was it Clare? Was she alive? Maybe they were firing at her corpse. He couldn't even consider the prospect.

He'd never forgive himself if she died because of his crazy idea of getting rich. What had he even been thinking of? Things like that didn't happen to people like him. They worked at day-jobs and had wives and kids. What he'd have given for that as he watched the thickset thug survey the waters once again before heading back towards the boat that was moored alongside the platform.

Matt could feel himself being washed out to sea. As he was thrown around in the water, he looked towards the boat ahead. The mooring area was right in front of him. It was an iron platform at sea level connected to the rest of the structure by a long staircase and punctuated by two platforms which ran around the fort's exterior. It was how the other guests would have boarded earlier. If he could only reach that, he'd be able to pull himself up and onto the fort.

Matt had a target now, he knew where he was heading. He turned himself around, pointing towards the boarding platform. The boat was the vessel that had let those bastards on board to terrorise them all. A bunch of rich people stuck out at sea with nobody to protect them – it was the perfect opportunity, and who better to target than Sebastian Helix, one of the world's wealthiest men.

Knowing how far he had to swim helped to re-energise Matt. It was more than that 100-metre swim at school, but he was certain that he could do it. The last time he'd been in the sea was a holiday in Spain. He'd been turned on by the way the water was making Clare's bikini cling to her breasts while they messed around in the calm blue water. It hadn't been the best training for his current dilemma.

He tried swimming on his back to conserve his energy, but the waves were too fierce. He panicked every time they threw him upwards. He'd have to swim against the force of the water. It was like trying to wade through mud. His clothes were sodden and weighty. The waves were relentless, his ears filled with the roar of the sea. It was so cold. His whole body was shaking.

The only way he could mark his progress was from the lights surrounding the fort. It was difficult to judge, but he seemed to be getting closer and the surrounding water was becoming better lit. And that's when he saw them: round pink objects bobbing around him in the waves. Jellyfish.

He tried not to thrash around so much as he made his way through them, but he had to keep afloat and drive himself forward. If he didn't continue to move towards the landing platform, he'd soon be dead. Then they came, the inevitable stings, like an assault from a wasp but many times worse. First on his arm, then on his leg. Matt tried to ignore the pain, but it was persistent and nagging. He was desperate to stop and rub it.

His strokes were getting weaker now, his progress slower. The boat was only metres ahead of him. A shot rang out. It was to the right of him, on the far side of the fort. Was it Clare? Had they found her? Torches were being shone from the side of the helipad, and another one from the mooring area. He ducked his head under the water to avoid being caught in the beam.

As he rose up again, he got caught in a wave and,

expecting to find air, took a massive gulp of water instead. He tried to choke it out, but was hit by another crashing wave. He struggled to reach the surface, his lungs screaming for oxygen, the stings stiffening his limbs and making every movement a battle. He couldn't breathe. Above him he could see the beam of a torch searching the surface of the water.

He had to take a breath. He could contain it no longer, he was about to pass out. He knew that his time was nearly up. A stillness was beginning to overcome him, a knowledge that death was almost upon him and that it wasn't as bad as he'd feared. Semi-conscious now, he moved his arms in one last feeble effort to propel himself to the surface. It was calm under the water, much easier than fighting the waves.

Clare must be dead. If she hadn't died in the fall, they'd probably shot her in the water. He'd dared to think he could make a better life for them. He'd stuck his head above the parapet and made his best effort at digging them out of their mediocre life. Well, he'd messed it up. They'd had one last chance to put things right. He'd put the love of his life in mortal danger and it had ended in disaster. It had been a deadly error, for both of them. Helix could take his idea, he didn't care anymore. Without Clare it was all pointless anyway. As the water filled his lungs, he gave himself up to his fate and let the sea take him.

CHAPTER TWENTY-FOUR

October, Helix Fort

Matt coughed and then retched several times. One minute his lungs had felt as if they were full of concrete, and then completely free the next. He sucked in the air, beautiful fresh air, it felt glorious. He was dazed and out of it, but slowly, despite being in some considerable pain, his mind began to sharpen.

'Bloody hell, Clare. You survived. Either that or this is heaven!'

Clare reached down and hugged him hard. She was wearing a blue coverall and her hair was tied back. She looked dishevelled but very much alive and well. They were on a boat which was rocking furiously.

'What happened?'

Matt was still feeling his way back into being able to breathe freely again. He was naked, wrapped in a blanket, and Clare was applying something to his leg.

'I saved your arse, that's what! But we're not out of the woods yet. Those bastards are still on the fort.'

Matt looked around, and then pulled himself bolt upright on the seat which had been supporting him.

'Jesus Christ, Clare. Did you do that?'

On the floor of the boat was the corpse of a man who looked like he'd enjoyed too many dinners in his lifetime. He had a harpoon spear through his head.

'It was him or me, and it wasn't going to be me. And yes, that's my vomit too. As it turns out it's easy to kill someone who's trying to kill you, but straight afterwards you're petrified and want to run away and hide. But we can't do that, right? These killers are after you, Matt, and your pen drive, and they're not going to stop until they get it.'

Matt sank back down onto the seat. His leg and arm stung like crazy and his lungs felt like a balloon that had been over-inflated. Clare was putting some cream on the jellyfish stings. It was helping. He was beginning to feel human again.

'I can't believe what's happening, Matt. This is the UK, I didn't think we had pirates here.'

'They must have known that all these rich people were gathered here. If you think about it, it's the perfect target: no police, nowhere to hide and the perfect getaway route. I should have thought about it myself – it might have made me a bit more money than I've earned in the past twelve months.'

'Don't you get it?' Clare stopped and looked at him. 'It's your idea they're after. Sure, they've taken every bit of jewellery that they can find, but they're still up there because of you. What the hell is it you created?'

'I can't believe this is all about my idea. If that's the case, maybe we should just let them have it and get it over with.'

'It's not as simple as that. I don't think anybody is walking off this fort alive. *No witnesses*, that's what I heard them say. They've already begun shooting the staff. I saw them throw one off the helipad. And do you think I'm still supposed to be here? They were shooting at me in the water. They're pissed off with you for jumping, though. They wanted to catch you alive.'

'What makes you so sure they're going to kill everybody?'

'Didn't you see what happened to Jerry? They put his finger in the middle of the table for us all to see. It bled out across the tablecloth as we sat there in silence. Sebastian has been beaten up badly. They moved him into a separate area. Who knows what they've done to him?'

Matt closed his eyes. For an instant he thought it would have been simpler to drown. Alive, he'd have to figure out a plan. They'd have to do something. He didn't want that responsibility. It felt safe on the boat. He just wanted a few more minutes with his wife before they did whatever it was they decided to do.

'Thanks for rescuing me, Clare. How did you do it?'

'You always were a bad swimmer!' she grinned. 'Once I'd recovered from the shock of going over the edge, I did the same as you. I headed for the landing platform. It's the only way to access the fort from the sea. Fortunately I didn't run into the jellyfish.

'I made it to the back of the boat and saw that Mr Blobby here was getting ready to shoot at something. Turns out it was you. Anyway, I threw a bucket at him to draw his fire, and then hid on the boat. Luckily I found the harpoon before he saw me. I shot him and swam out to rescue you. You were completely out when I reached you. I had to practise my best secondary school lifesaving moves. Oh, and you need to lose weight. You're far too heavy to drag around. At least you were able to stagger after I got the worst of the water out of you.'

Matt couldn't even recall that bit. He'd come around in the boat not out on the iron platform. A walkie-talkie crackled somewhere in the distance.

'Don't tell me ... this is only a partial rescue, right?'

'Right. You need to get a pair of those overalls on and take his shoes – he doesn't need them anymore.'

He saw that she was putting on a brave face.

'You don't need to feel guilty about it,' he said. 'You had to kill him. I've killed three of them now. I didn't have a choice. Nor did you.'

'I know. But I feel sick, guilty, terrified ... I can't believe I did that to him.'

'If you hadn't, I'd be dead now. Or you would. Even worse, neither of us would be here. We had to do it, Clare. We have to do whatever it takes to walk away from this. We didn't start it.'

Matt was stiff and sore. He'd have been quite happy to lie back down on the seat for a couple of days. He could hear a voice on a walkie-talkie. They were paging their colleague. When he didn't respond, they'd come straight down to the boat. He and Clare had to be ready.

'Have you got a plan, Clare? Perhaps we could take the boat, drive it back to shore and raise the alarm.'

'No keys! But even if we could get this thing going, I'm not sure we'd get it across the water with the waves like this.'

'I'd take my chances.'

Matt had pulled on the overalls and was putting on the dead man's shoes. They weren't such a bad fit, and it was certainly better than going barefoot.

'We've got the harpoon and one gun. Oh, and you had

two flares hanging out of your pocket, Matt. I don't know if they need to be dry, but they look alright. That should be enough to protect ourselves. How many of them were there?'

'I've lost count. There was one left on the helipad and some others with the guests. I've killed three of them and we've got this chap here too. That's four down. Oh, and Eddy. Did you see Eddy? He's out there somewhere with a gun. I reckon he must be security or ex-special forces, something like that. We need to find him. He'll be able to help. He may even have alerted the police.'

Matt could see from his wife's face that she'd completely forgotten about Eddy.

The walkie-talkie was alive with chatter now. They were calling the dead man. His name was Pete.

'Come in, Pete. Answer! Come on, you fat git. If you're taking another shit, I'll haul you out of there myself and throw you into the sea.'

'One last try,' Matt said. 'Is there a proper radio on this boat? Not a walkie-talkie like that, I mean a proper one for the boat.'

'They brought it with them. The guy who's in charge – Baptiste – has been using it on the fort. He's chatting away to somebody or other. I had a quick look around when I was looking for the first aid box. All we can use is what I told you about already.'

'Okay, Clare, you take the gun. I'll have the harpoon and we'll take a flare each. I must have lost a flare in the water, I'm sure I had three. We need to get back onto the main structure. Did you get a good look at the platforms when you were in the water? Are there stairs all the way around the fort or just this main set?'

'I didn't see. I know what you're thinking: it would be

best to work around the edge and enter the fort where they're not expecting us. There's not many of them left now, they can't be everywhere. And we have an advantage. They don't know we're alive – that is until they find Pete here. At least we'll have some small element of surprise.'

'Okay, let's go, they'll be down here soon.'

Matt paused. He looked at Clare and she sensed he had something important to say.

'What?'

'You know I would never willingly have betrayed you. That night, with Victoria … I can't explain it. I would never have done that.'

'We'll talk about it later – if we ever get out of this mess, that is. Right now we need to stop talking and make a move. If we get trapped on the platform, they've got us, and the only way out is the sea. I'm not doing that again.'

The walkie-talkie was silent now. Matt guessed that one of the hired thugs would report Pete's lack of a response to Baptiste who would send one or two of the men down to investigate. They'd be running out of men soon, and there were a lot of people to guard. Still, one gun would be enough in a room of terrified people. None of them would risk getting shot.

Then Matt saw how the situation was being managed. About a hundred yards away a body dressed in chef's whites came flying off the edge of the fort. His head struck one of the iron railings and then his lifeless form splashed into the sea. That was followed by three shots and another two bodies. That was all three members of the waiting team now dead, including the body that Clare had seen earlier. They were clearing the helipad. And the catering staff had evidently just been deemed expendable.

CHAPTER TWENTY-FIVE

October, Helix Fort

'We have to go, Matt ... Matt!'

Clare was shouting at him. He'd always known his wife was strong, but seeing her now, she was incredible. She led the way and he followed, trying desperately to recover his strength. The spray from the sea was soaking them, but the higher they climbed up the iron steps the easier it would be. Matt was in a lot of pain, his joints stiffened by the stings, and his breathing still hadn't returned to normal. It felt as if there wasn't enough air to go around. His lungs had been flooded with water. He was bound to be woozy – he was lucky he hadn't sustained any brain damage from the lack of oxygen.

Clare pulled him to one side.

'There are two of them working their way down from the top. We need to keep into the side and get to the first platform before they do.'

They upped their pace, leaping two or three stairs at a

time, desperate to reach the first platform. If they could do that, and get far enough along it to be concealed from view by the curvature of the structure, they'd be in with a chance.

They reached the first level.

'Wait!' Clare said. 'Let them get to the second platform. When they start to walk down the stairs, we'll take the opportunity to run out of sight while they're facing away from us. You know I said you've put on weight? Now is the time to start losing it!'

They watched and waited, poised and ready to run.

'Okay, go!'

Matt estimated there would be ten to fifteen steps until the men were facing them directly. They started to sprint, using the circular design to their advantage. He was completely out of condition and hindered by the harpoon he was carrying in his hand. Clare was way ahead of him.

'It's okay. We can stop now. We're clear.'

She came to a halt and Matt stopped beside her. They were both out of breath, but they'd made it. The two men would find Pete dead on the boat, and then raise the alarm.

'They'll assume only one of us survived,' Matt said, his heart pounding. 'I was the one who ran and jumped so they'll think it was me.'

'You're right. They'll think it was you who killed Pete. I'm still not sure how I managed to save myself and you as well. They'll think I'm dead. We'll have to play that to our advantage. We have to split up.'

'No way. I'm not leaving you again.'

'Matt! We have to. You saw how they were treating me up there. I'm not leaving Kylie on her own to deal with that. We're going to help those people. And we're going to raise the alarm.'

Matt knew she was right. He wished he was as in

control as she was. He couldn't get his head straight. Perhaps the fall into the water had affected him more than he thought. He tried to focus.

'Okay, and look, we should shoot these flares. We don't want to give our whereabouts away, but someone might see them – the lifeguard perhaps, they'll be active around here.'

'Good idea,' said Clare. 'I'll release mine from the opposite side of the fort to the boat. It only takes one nosey person to alert the police or the coastguard. We need to take the lead though, disorientate these madmen and pick them off, one-by-one.'

'You mean kill them?' Matt said. 'When you say "pick them off" you mean kill them, right?'

'What else can we do?' Clare hissed at him. 'I don't want to use this damn gun, but they haven't given me a choice. We must do this, Matt. We can't let those innocent people die up there.'

'Okay, okay, I know, but I hate being forced into this. What if I just give them the pen drive?'

'You really think they'll let us walk away? After what we've seen tonight there's no way they're going to let us get off this fort alive. It's us or them.'

'You're right, but we need a plan.'

'Did you see the generators when we were on the tour of the fort? I think we should shut them down. It'll plunge the place into semi-darkness – there'll only be the safety lights left on. If we can create some confusion, we might be able to separate them. If we can link up with Eddy, it'll almost be a level game. There can only be four or five of them left now.'

'I'll do the generator. I don't want you getting trapped below the deck. Why don't you start a fire somewhere? Get the smoke alarms going. We can try and get some of them out of the dining room while they're checking it out.'

'Since they came for your pen drive, it might be a good idea to have it on you. We might be able to try for a trade with them.'

'You're right. I'll get it on the way to the generators. If we make a mess of things, let's try and meet up back here. It's out of the way. There's a door along this walkway into the main building.'

Matt reached out to hug his wife. He pulled her in close. This might be the last time he saw her.

'I'm going to set off this flare, then head for the second staircase and up to the deck. Take care, Matt.'

Matt turned and headed towards the door, the harpoon still in his hand. The door was heavy and firm, the sort that you'd find on a ship. It was unlocked. Why wouldn't it be? Nobody would be expecting thieves so far out at sea.

It was quiet along the curving corridor. Matt swiftly recognised where he was and headed for their bedroom, moving stealthily and hugging the wall to give himself as much cover as he could. He stopped and listened outside the open door. Nothing. He walked inside. They'd ransacked it once again. He began to sweat as he rushed over to the mattress, which had been thrown against the window. He dropped the harpoon onto the rug. Had they found it?

He inserted his fingers in the hole. Nothing. He pushed down on the mattress, feeling for a small lump. Yes, it was there! It had worked its way deeper into the filling as the mattress had been thrown around the room. He'd got it, his one bargaining chip.

Then, just to his side, he heard a footstep. Matt turned

around, cursing that he'd dropped the harpoon. He relaxed immediately when he saw who it was.

'Eddy, thank God. I thought it was one of them! Where have you been? Jeez, am I please to see you—'

'Stay where you are.'

Eddy kicked the harpoon out of the way. He was pointing his gun at Matt.

'Eddy, it's me, we can deal with these guys together—'

'Shut up, you arsehole!'

Eddy moved up close to him, placing his gun to Matt's temple.

'Now give me that pen drive so we can all get off this wretched fort!'

CHAPTER TWENTY-SIX

October, Helix Fort

The sensation of the gun pressing against his temple was unnerving. One squeeze of that trigger and it could be over in a second. His behaviour might have been a little reckless that evening, but Matt didn't want to die. Like Eddy, he wanted to get off that cursed fort and back to safety. With Clare.

'Okay, okay, you can have the pen drive!'

He looked around for something that could help to extricate him from his current predicament. The harpoon was too far away to be of any use. Besides, he didn't want to kill Eddy. This confrontation didn't seem to be part of the drama going on elsewhere on the fort.

'What's this about, Eddy? You're not anything to do with what's been going on tonight, are you?'

'Just give me the pen drive, Mr Dalton, and cut the patter. I really don't want to hurt you, but I've got to secure the asset now. Hand it over.'

'You know that Clare is in danger up there, don't you? She's a civilian in all this, she only came along to support me this weekend. You're not a bad man, Eddy. I know that. I don't think you want to see her harmed.'

'You need to shut up, Mr Dalton. I see you've retrieved the pen drive. Hand it over. Please don't make me take it from you.'

Matt considered his options. There weren't many. He could try to run for it. Good luck with that. He'd expended too much energy already and didn't reckon on his chances of out-running a bullet. He could make a dash for the harpoon. Again, not the cleverest of moves.

He still couldn't place Eddy. He was polite and in control; he had to have done this sort of thing before. Police maybe? Military perhaps? There was something about him. Matt was not going to be deceived by the fact that he was in his mid-to-late fifties. Eddy was trim and could clearly handle himself. He'd have one more try to connect with him.

'How about we work on this together?' he suggested. 'We both want to get Sebastian out of this mess – I take it he is still your boss. We can work as a team, you'll be a hero if we get out of this alive.'

Matt's hand moved down to his pocket. He'd realised he did have another option.

Suddenly there was the loud crack of a gunshot and Eddy fell backwards. In the doorway stood one of the men he'd seen earlier standing guard in the dining room. He was now pointing his gun at Matt. Matt looked into his eyes. He knew they wanted the pen drive – there was no way they were going to shoot him. They needed him alive.

He drew the flare out of his back pocket and unscrewed the lid, tugging at the tag at the top of it. He'd expected it to shoot out like a rocket but instead it began to emit orange smoke like the world's most disappointing Roman candle. He dropped it onto the floor.

The room soon filled with a thick fog. Both Matt and his attacker began to cough and splutter. He scooped his hand down to retrieve the harpoon from the floor but couldn't find it. He staggered through the smoke, pushing past the gunman and out of the door. He had to get out of there fast if the flare was going to give him any kind of an advantage.

He sprinted along the curving corridor and careered down the iron staircase towards the basement. He had to get to the lower levels where the generators were located. Clare would be relying on him.

As he neared the bottom of the staircase, he heard the door above him closing. He was being pursued. Of course he was. It was only a little smoke – a cough and splutter wasn't going to deter these killers from getting what they'd come for. He scanned the area, trying to recall where the generators were. The footsteps were close. He chose a direction – any direction.

He was in the bowels of the fort in a circular corridor with low doors at regular intervals on either side. When the fort had been built the rooms would have been used for barracks and storage, nowadays Helix used the area for paintball. Dotted along the white-painted brick walls were the pinks, greens and blues of paintball pellets. A millionaire's play area. He and Clare barely had room in their house to store the recycling bags.

His only choice was to play cat and mouse, to dodge in and out of the rooms and either get ahead – or behind – the man who was hunting him. Matt did a count in his head. He'd lost track of how many armed men there were on the fort. He'd not had the chance to see them all together. He reckoned three, maybe four now.

He'd been shocked by how fast Eddy had been thrown back when the bullet hit him. Matt hadn't had time to turn and see what his injuries were, but he'd been aware of him moving behind him when the flare went off. For all he knew, he'd taken a second or third bullet as Matt had escaped from the room.

Quietly he began to move along the corridor. It felt solid and oppressive down there – the upper levels were so light and airy. He passed the table on which paintball guns, pellets and protective gear were laid out. He grabbed a handful of pellets and a gun and began to jog to put some distance between him and the man behind him.

There were so many doors, right and left, it was disorientating. Some were closed and padlocked, but the majority were open and the rooms empty. Matt ducked into one and started to load his ridiculous weapon. He knew it was no match for a real gun, but if he fired it at the guy's face he might at least be able to make an escape. Another escape. It wasn't lost on Matt that he was giving the proverbial cat-with-nine-lives a run for its money. He couldn't get cocky. Clare was waiting for him. It wasn't just him who had to survive. He had to keep Clare safe too.

He could hear cautious footsteps along the corridor. He'd seen the movies. His pursuer would be scouring the rooms, finger on trigger, alert and ready to shoot.

'Mr Dalton, my name is Noah ...'

French. Definitely a French accent. Matt's language GCSE hadn't been a time-waster after all. He waited. Noah was trying to flush him out, he wasn't daft.

'We have your wife, Mr Dalton. She has a great pair of

tits. I'm keeping her for myself. She's a beautiful looking woman. Shame she's going to be a widow soon.'

Matt felt sick. Had they got Clare again? If they'd captured her, they had him over a barrel. His instinct was to shout back.

'I hope you don't mind, Mr Dalton, but I ran my hand over her tight ass. That's a beautiful piece of ass, I'll bet you're very sorry you'll never get to look at that again.'

Matt could hear the voice getting closer. He wanted to smash the bastard's head in, but he had to wait for his moment. A move too soon and he'd give away his where-abouts, placing Clare in even more peril.

'I need the pen drive, Mr Dalton. This was supposed to be a nice and easy job. I can't tell you how pissed I am about what happened here tonight. That's why I'm going to take out my stress on your lovely wife. I can't wait to get myself some of that beautiful woman.'

Matt had only played paintball once. He was terrible at it and ended up looking like a walking Picasso painting. He remembered that the pellets gave quite a kick and he'd been thankful for the protective gear that they'd been given. A few shots of this weapon would buy him some getaway time.

The footsteps were almost upon him now. All he had was the element of surprise. Noah gave a cough. He must have been suffering the after-effects of the smoke from the flare. He was just outside the door.

Matt moved towards the back of the small room, finding as much cover in the shadows as he could. He waited, tensed for action, the paintball gun pointing directly towards the door.

He heard Noah move quickly into the doorway opposite.

'Hurry up, Mr Dalton. Your wife won't wait forever. It's high time she got her hands on a real man—'

Matt coughed. That bloody smoke had caught him now. Immediately alerted, Noah appeared in the doorway, his gun sweeping the room ready to find its target. It was the man with the scarred face, the one who'd tried to intimidate Clare. Still coughing, Matt drew up the paintball gun and prepared to shoot. It was the most ludicrous gun draw ever. But if Matt couldn't disable his target, he was a dead man.

CHAPTER TWENTY-SEVEN

October, Helix Fort

Matt fired as fast as the paintball gun would release its pellets. He landed an early shot on Noah's face. Noah fired his revolver – once, twice then a third time. He was taking potshots, thrashing around, trying to hit a target that he couldn't see.

Then ... nothing. Only the click of a paintball gun and no pellet released. Noah had been hit several times. For a moment he was thrown off his stride but he wouldn't be deterred for long.

There was silence. Matt looked at the shit who'd been threatening his wife. He wanted to beat the crap out of him. Covered in fluorescent liquid, Noah wiped his face and levelled his gun. Matt moved back, trying to melt into the wall, but he was cornered like a rat. He had no tricks left, there was nothing else to do but wait for the bullet.

'I'm going to take that pen drive from your pocket and

then I'm going to screw your wife. But first I'm going to shoot you through the head.'

He was taking his time. He knew he'd got Matt exactly where he wanted him. For the second time that night, Matt relaxed, just as he had when he'd been on the verge of drowning. It was crazy. He was about to die, but there comes a point when there's nothing more you can do.

He loved Clare, he always had, despite their current issues. What was it they called it ... First World problems? Well, that's what he and Clare had. There was nothing that couldn't have been sorted out between them. But it was too late now.

Matt saw Noah back out of the doorway, his finger ready to squeeze the trigger. He never figured out why he did that. Perhaps it was to protect his ears from the sound of the gunshot. Matt closed his eyes in expectation of the bullet. 'I love you, Clare,' he whispered. 'I'm sorry I couldn't do better.'

The shot didn't come. There was a swishing, metallic sound to the left along the corridor. Noah dropped his gun and Matt opened his eyes in time to see him sink to the ground, a harpoon dart through his head. On his face was an expression of shock, as if somebody had sprung a surprise party on him.

Matt stood up to his full height. He hadn't realised how bowed over he'd been as he'd stood with his eyes closed awaiting the inevitable. He could hear a shuffling sound from further up the corridor. Friend or foe? Matt was tiring now; the surges of adrenalin were beginning to take their toll. He peered cautiously around the doorway. There, bloodied and grimacing in pain, was Eddy.

Matt dropped the paintball gun and looked into his eyes.

'Are we good?' he asked, scanning the floor for Noah's gun, just in case Eddy was going to force him to use it.

Eddy stopped and returned his look. For a moment, Matt wasn't sure which way this was going.

Eddy nodded.

'We're good,' he said. 'I'm going to need your help. But I can see you're not involved in this, I'm sorry I doubted you. But I don't really know you - I thought you might have been responsible for what happened here tonight. I'm sorry, you just saved my life back there with your little flare trick. So, let's work together to get the other guests out of here alive.'

Matt felt a massive sense of relief. It was bad enough killing anonymous bad guys. He had no wish to fight Eddy who seemed to be a decent guy trying to look after the interests of his boss. He couldn't blame him for being suspicious.

'We need to get to the generators. Clare's waiting for me.'

He thought back to what Noah had said. Did they really have Clare again, or had he been taunting Matt to get him to show himself?

'We can do that later. We have to alert the police. It takes half an hour to get a boat out here – helicopter is quicker, but they'll need an armed response team.'

'Haven't you done that already?' Matt asked, as if Eddy had all the answers.

'No mobile phone signal,' Eddy answered. 'The weather's too bad now. And communications have been disabled. Someone knows how this place operates. If the police approach the fort, we'll end up in a hostage situation. It's called a fort for a good reason. Nobody gets on or off without somebody knowing about it.'

Matt hadn't considered a hostage scenario. They could be stuck on the fort for days. With high-value hostages like

Sebastian Helix, great care would need to be taken. The police couldn't just blunder onto the fort like the cavalry arriving in the nick of time.

'What do you think is going on?' he asked, a little embarrassed that he hadn't thought things through.

'I don't know. These guys, they're operating like pirates. They seem to be hired hands, doing somebody else's dirty work for them, but I don't know who's behind it. They're French, as you probably realise. Something has been awry for some weeks now, but I haven't been able to put my finger on what it is.'

His face contorted in pain. He'd been shot in the leg and had lost a lot of blood.

'Can I bandage that wound?' Matt asked. 'At least I can try to stop the blood loss. You're no good to me passed out.'

Eddy nodded and slumped against the wall in the small room where Matt had been hiding. Undeterred by the harpoon dart through Noah's head, Matt removed the dead man's belt and did his best to fasten it securely around Eddy's leg.

'Did you see what they did to Jerry?' he asked as he picked up Noah's discarded gun and placed it at Eddy's side.

'I was watching from the kitchen. That journalist – Kylie – she created a tourniquet to stop the bleeding and even got them to put the finger in the freezer. She's got balls that one. She shouted at them until they let her do it. Could easily have got herself shot. Your wife was helping too.'

'That's really good to hear.' Matt paused. Then he asked, 'Didn't you realise I wasn't involved in any of this?'

'None of it rings true to me. I don't know what to believe. We're in the Solent, not offshore from Somalia. This sort of shit doesn't happen in the UK.'

'And what about my pen drive? What's the big deal about that? I know it's got potential to make a lot of money, but why this level of interest? Is it really worth killing people for?'

'I don't know. My job is to keep Sebastian Helix safe and protect his interests. Your pen drive is one of his interests. Speaking of which, I take it you still have it?'

Matt nodded.

'And would you let me take it now, so I can put it somewhere a little safer than a mattress in your bedroom?'

Matt hesitated. Was anywhere safe on the fort?

'Let's wait a while, shall we? You're not in such a good way yourself. Besides, I need to build a bit of trust of my own. You had a gun to my head not a quarter of an hour ago.'

There was silence. Matt thought he saw Eddy's hand creeping towards his gun, but he obviously thought better of it.

'Look Eddy, our priority is to make sure that everybody is safe and to get these bastards off the fort. We need to figure out the best way to do that. I still think the generator idea is good. Do you know how many of them are left now?'

'Two. That's all. Both have guns. Once they realise Noah here is dead, they'll start to panic. They'll want to get off, but they won't leave without your pen drive. This isn't about jewellery and Rolex watches.'

'Okay, so we have a bargaining chip. Maybe we can set things up – exchange the pen drive for the hostages. The police will catch them anyway, won't they?'

Eddy considered that one.

'It's difficult to tell. They might head for the mainland. They could travel via the Isle of Wight – if they have a light aircraft at their disposal, they could fly out to France. My guess is that's how they'll make their escape. They'll be away before the police even know they were here.

'These guys are mercenaries, they're hired hands sent in to do someone's dirty work. They don't give a toss who they hurt and how they achieve their objective. Their payday comes when they deliver their payload, whatever that is. They're as likely to put a bullet through your head as they are to do a deal. Once they've got what they wanted, they'll disappear into the background. Nobody will know who they are. Most of them have a wife and children back home.'

'You seem to know a lot about all this.'

'I haven't always been a middle-aged security consultant, you know. Sebastian Helix needs more than a former PC Plod looking after him. Do you realise how vulnerable you are if you have that much money?'

Matt had never really thought about it. Now Eddy mentioned it, the threat of kidnapping, ransom or extortion must be constant for Sebastian. It was an unfamiliar world to Matt and one which was becoming increasingly less attractive. Suddenly, his mundane life with Clare in their modest house seemed to be the most attractive option. He'd be careful what he wished for in future.

Without warning, the lights went out plunging them into darkness for a moment before the safety lights flickered on. They were barely sufficient to see by – they could only just make out the side of the walls.

'It must be Clare,' Matt said. 'She must have shut down the generator on her own. Noah was lying. We have to go to her and finish this together.'

CHAPTER TWENTY-EIGHT

October, Helix Fort

Eddy slowly got to his feet. Matt's patch-up job seemed to have done the trick. The bleeding had stopped and the blood was beginning to dry out on his trousers.

'One gun each,' Matt said, picking up the weapon that Noah had been wielding. 'Any idea how many bullets we have between us?'

Eddy examined the magazines.

'You want the good news or the bad news?'

'The bad news.'

'I have one bullet left. That's it. One more shot and I'm out of the game.'

'What was the good news?'

'You have three bullets left. Why do you think I used the harpoon on that guy? I had a clear line of sight when he stepped back into the corridor, I wasn't wasting my last bullet.'

'Can you walk? Let's find Clare before she gets herself

into more trouble. They must know by now that Noah here has run into trouble. They'll be really pissed.'

Matt and Eddy headed off along the curving corridor. Eddy knew the way, even in the semi-darkness, and before long they were out on the lower deck, standing by the massive generators. They stepped cautiously out of the door, aware that Clare had a weapon and would probably be as jittery as they were.

'Clare! Clare!' Matt whispered.

No reply. Maybe she'd headed back to the upper deck.

'Clare? Are you here?'

Nothing.

'She must have gone. If she thinks I didn't make it, who knows how careless she'll be? If what you said is right, these guys are mercenaries and they'll eat her for breakfast.'

'Matt? Is that you?'

A figure stepped out of the darkness. He'd expected Clare. It was Victoria Winterton.

'Jesus, Victoria. You frightened the life out of me! Are you okay? How did you get out?'

Victoria stepped out from behind the generator into the glow of a safety light. She acknowledged Eddy, who seemed wary of her.

'Kylie and I got out when the lights went off – we made a run for it. Things are getting pretty tense in there. We could hear shots, but I don't know if anybody got hit. I've lost Kylie too. I don't know where she went.'

'Did they hurt anybody? How is Jerry?'

'Jerry's in a bad way, he's been out cold. Kylie and Clare managed to help him. Is Clare okay? They took her outside, but I don't know what they did to her.'

'It's a long story. She's okay. We were coming to meet her in the basement, but what are you doing here?'

Victoria paused.

'It's the safest place to hide. You can squeeze behind the generators. I thought you were one of them.'

'Who turned the generator off? It must have been Clare.'

'If it was, I'm grateful. I wouldn't have got away if she hadn't done that. Have you two got a plan to rescue us?'

Eddy stayed quiet. Matt broke the silence.

'This was the plan: turn off the power and try to draw them out, letting at least some of the hostages get away.'

'You do know it's you they're after?' Victoria said.

Matt nodded.

'Yes. I know they want to get their hands on the rest of my idea, but surely it isn't worth all this?'

'We should clear this area,' Eddy said. 'They might come down to investigate. How are they guarding the hostages, Victoria?'

'They're still seated around the table, chairs pulled in tight. There's one guy – Alby – with a machine gun trained on everybody. Olaf has pissed himself twice now.'

'Is Mr Helix there too?'

'No, they're keeping him separate. He's restrained in the cloakroom area.'

'How come you and Kylie got out?'

'They were letting us get some water from the bar. It was Kylie's suggestion. People were getting thirsty and Vinden had a pill to take. The guy in charge – Baptiste or whatever his name is – had a gun on us all the time. When the lights went off, we didn't hang around. We were off like a shot.'

'What about Kylie?'

'I don't know. I ran left, she ran right. Baptiste was coming after us, there was no time for a strategy meeting.'

'At least you're safe. Do you have any idea what's going on?'

'You know you're patient zero, right? Whatever it is you have on that pen drive of yours, they want it. And whoever they're talking to on that radio of theirs is really pissed off with you. Let's put it this way, you just got crossed off the Christmas card list.'

Matt thought it over. There were only two of the gang left. They were outnumbered, but at least they knew how many they were dealing with now. They could do this between them, even with no bullets or training.

'What are you thinking, Eddy? Draw them out, take them out one at a time?'

Eddy looked unsure.

'This still isn't working for me,' he replied. 'First I want to know who's on the other end of that radio. I want to know who's behind this. We need to tread carefully—'

'They were getting ready to leave,' Victoria interrupted. 'The catering staff are all dead now. Baptiste had them moving the jewellery haul out onto the top deck before they threw them over the edge.'

'They're in a boat, aren't they?' asked Matt.

'It doesn't look like they're leaving on a boat,' Victoria replied. 'I'd say they're travelling by helicopter.'

'It's what I thought,' Eddy said. 'A boat is too slow. They'd get caught at sea – aircraft is much easier. They'll just disappear into the night. Bastards.'

'You've got the pen drive, Matt?' Victoria asked. 'It's still safe, isn't it?'

'Yes. It's still safe.'

Matt touched his pocket. It was an instinctive move, making sure it was still there.

'You've got it on you?' Her eyes widened. 'That's a bit dangerous, isn't it?'

'Again, it's a long story!' Matt replied. 'I figure it's the only leverage we've got.'

As he finished speaking, he became aware of a noise off in the distance. It took a few seconds to realise what it was. The weather was wild, the cold wind howled around the uncovered centre of the fort. But with the generator now quiet, he could just make out a chopping sound far off, out at sea.

'You hear that?'

'It's a helicopter,' Eddy said, straining to make out the sound. 'I'm sure it is. Who the hell is that ... not the police chopper, surely?'

They looked up from the centre of the fort into the dark skies. They saw the blades first, then the helicopter.

'That's Tucker, isn't it? Or Sebastian's helicopter, at least. We need to warn him. He doesn't know what he'll be walking into. He'll get himself killed!'

Matt spun around, ready to head back up the staircase and out onto the top deck where he'd do what he could to warn Tucker. Much as he would be relieved to see a friendly face, Tucker couldn't land there, it was too dangerous.

He realised how naive he'd been at the precise moment that Baptiste stepped out of the shadows. Without hesitation, he struck Eddy on the head with the butt of his pistol, and then dexterously spun it around so that it was trained on Matt.

Victoria stepped aside.

'Nicely done, Victoria. Two cockroaches in one trap.' He turned to Matt. 'You have been a pain in the arse this evening, Mr Dalton, but I'm pleased to say that we can now leave this godforsaken fort. It's a good job that pen drive is worth it. You've just made me a very rich man. Get it out of your pocket and kindly hand it to Ms Winterton.'

As he was speaking, Victoria darted in and grabbed Matt's gun. Matt didn't resist, he knew there was no play to make here. They'd got him. Everything had just become more sharply focused. Victoria was in on it. Eddy clearly wasn't. And whoever was piloting that helicopter had come to whisk them away, probably as Eddy had guessed to the Isle of Wight, and then they would disappear into thin air with a haul of valuable jewellery and his pen drive.

'That was a set-up?' Matt asked. 'You and me in that hotel room?'

'Jesus, yes! Don't worry, Matt. We didn't fuck that night. You're not my sort anyway. It was just a little diversion for your lovely wife Clare.'

'Did you really get out with Kylie, or was that a lie too?'

'Really, Matt? You're slow to catch on. It was all bollocks. We're done here now. It's time to go. Now, the pen drive please.'

'What about Clare and the others? What happens now you've got what you came for?'

'You're a little bastard, you know that, Matt? I thought I'd got a copy of your idea that night after I slipped a sedative in your coffee, but it turns out you're a smart-arse and split the code. I had to leave the event once you told me your wife was away so that we could break into your house and see if we could find it there. I hope you noticed that we didn't damage your front door when we broke in. You should thank us for leaving your house so tidy. But enough of that ... The pen drive, please.'

Matt took it out of his pocket and handed it to her.

Baptiste was watching everything, poised for him to make a move.

'Thank you.' Victoria showed it to Baptiste, as if to confirm it was real.

'You didn't answer my question. What happens to us now: Clare, Eddy, the others?'

'For someone who's so clever, you don't half catch on slowly. Baptiste, do you want to put him out of his misery? Bearing in mind this little heist is worth at least three million euros.'

Baptiste's eyes narrowed. He had a sneering look, he knew that he held all the cards. Above them, out on the main deck, the helicopter landed.

Baptiste spoke, his voice almost drowned out by the sound of the chopper above.

'We leave no trace,' he began. 'No clues, no witnesses, no loose ends. You're all going into the sea. Every one of you.'

CHAPTER TWENTY-NINE

October, Helix Fort

The blades of the helicopter were still running as they stepped out onto the top deck. The helipad was bright and well lit, in contrast to the semi-darkness inside. Matt tried to see who was piloting the machine. There was no sign of Clare. She must have been the one who'd turned off the power. She was out there somewhere, watching.

Eddy had rallied since his blow to the head and was able to walk. He'd been relieved of his weapon so they were both defenceless now. Baptiste was waving the machine gun around recklessly. Clare wouldn't stand a chance against something like that. She had to stay safe. Perhaps she would end up as the sole witness to what had happened on Helix Fort.

Matt considered the scene that would be discovered there. Sooner or later somebody would come to the fort. They'd probably arrive by boat, perhaps with supplies, and they'd wonder why the place was so quiet. They would find it abandoned, traces of blood and violence all over. Unless Clare somehow managed to stay hidden, there'd be nobody left to tell the tale. Victoria, Baptiste and whoever else was involved would have fled, and the investigating teams would be left with a mystery.

Matt was alert now, looking for any opportunity to break free and take the initiative. The numbers were no longer in their favour. Baptiste, Victoria and the thug called Alby were armed – there were two machine guns in the mix and Victoria had Eddy's gun with its three bullets.

Alby was leading the other hostages out onto the deck. They were clearly terrified. When they saw Eddy and Matt, for an instant their faces betrayed a glimmer of hope that there would be a way out of their predicament.

Quentin and Hunter were holding hands. They sensed what was going to happen but didn't want to scare the older members of the group. There was no sign of Jerry. Olaf had pissed himself again and Gina wanted to see the dogs. Sebastian Helix was nowhere to be seen. Victoria had said that he'd been kept separately.

This was it. It seemed incredible to Matt. They were in UK waters, and on a clear day they'd be able to see Portsmouth from where they were standing. And yet it was like being in a lawless country. There was nobody to respond to a shout for help, no phone to use – nothing. They were exposed and defenceless.

The helicopter was idling. This was it now. Matt could see the pilot getting out on the far side. He hoped it wasn't Tucker – he'd liked the man. How could his judgment be so wrong? But then he'd liked Victoria too. She'd seemed pleasant, professional, genial.

As they stood at the base of the helipad, guns trained on them, with no chance of escape, Matt caught sight of Clare hiding by the fire pit, which was still alight, not far from the hot tubs they'd been using earlier. It was deep and sunken, its coals glowing red, a spectacular feature. Had the evening gone as planned, they'd have been gathering around it for nightcaps now. This was the place Olaf Strauss had openly flirted with his wife. That all seemed so long ago now and so trivial.

The helicopter pilot stepped down from the platform. Matt was relieved it wasn't Tucker. He heard him call across to Baptiste. It was another Frenchman, but Matt didn't catch his name.

Clare caught his eye and put her finger to her lips. He tried not to make it obvious where he was looking. What was she going to do? She had four of them to overpower, and they had machine guns. She wouldn't stand a chance.

'What are we doing with this lot?' the pilot asked. 'I suggest we make a move now. The weather is a little better, and we want to be well clear of this place when daylight comes.'

Baptiste nodded towards the sea. The pilot knew what he meant. He was armed too, another machine gun. Eddy was right when he'd described these men as mercenaries; this was no amateur outfit. Weaponry like that took some sourcing. It wasn't the type of equipment you'd get your hands on via a guy in the pub you paid in goods you'd stolen from the back of a lorry.

'We need to move the bodies. They should go into the sea. By the time they're picked up they'll be more difficult to identify. It'll give us all the head start we need.'

'Use the young ones to carry them up here, but not Dalton,' said Victoria. 'Olaf, Quentin, Hunter and Kylie ... you're on. Go with Alby. You've got some carrying to do. Where did you leave Noah, Matt? I assume he's dead.'

Alby signalled to the group to move, but they paused to hear Matt's reply.

'Yes, you're right. He's dead. You'll find him in the lower corridor with a harpoon through his head.'

Olaf was snivelling now.

'Please don't hurt me,' he pleaded through his sobs. 'This wasn't in our deal. I'll give you the code for my idea. It's yours, if you just let me go. I don't want to die.'

'Your idea is a heap of crap, Olaf,' sneered Victoria. 'Sebastian told me as much himself. We ran some tests – your tech doesn't work and your pitch is fraudulent. You're all mouth and no trousers. Your idea is worthless to us.'

Olaf panicked. His one bargaining chip had suddenly been rendered useless.

'Wait! I do have one more thing to trade. If I tell you where Clare Dalton is hiding, will you let me go?'

'You little shit!' Matt lunged forward to punch him.

Baptiste trained his gun on Matt, who moved back immediately.

'Carry on talking,' Baptiste said, scanning the area, wondering where Clare might be concealed. She was their only loose end now. They needed her out of the way with the others.

'Keep your mouth shut!' Matt warned, but Olaf didn't care who he ratted out. He wanted to stay alive at any cost. He'd arrived at the fort in spectacular fashion but he had every intention of leaving in a boat like a regular visitor – warm and safe and alive.

'I need a guarantee. If I tell you where she is, you'll let me go. I won't tell anyone about you. I don't care. Just leave me here. I'll say it was thugs from the mainland and that I didn't get a look at their faces. I'll throw the police off the scent for you.'

Victoria smiled at Baptiste.

'Yeah, okay. Go for it, Olaf. Where is the bitch? You tell us where she is and we'll leave you locked up in the cloakroom. You can tell everybody you're a hero.'

'Thank you, thank you so much!' he said, stepping away from Kylie, Quentin and Hunter. 'She's up there by the fire pit. She's been watching us since we came out onto the deck. She's got a gun, so be careful.'

'Thanks for that.' Victoria nodded to the pilot. 'Yanis will handle things from here.'

Holding his gun to Olaf's back, Yanis grabbed his neck with his spare hand and started to march him towards the fire pit. Matt looked over to Clare. She was still there, clearly unsure what to do next.

Olaf was now crying and begging for his life. Yanis lifted him into the air and threw him face down into the red-hot embers. He screamed as his skin burned. His clothing started to smoke, and then burst into flames.

'That's enough!' Clare stood up from behind the far side of the pit, her gun in the air. 'Let him out. Please, just let him out!'

Yanis strode over to her and wrenched the gun from her hand. Olaf was still screaming, desperately trying to claw his way out of the deep pit. Yanis raised his gun, pointed it at Olaf's head and pulled the trigger. His body convulsed and fell lifeless in the centre of the fire, his clothes burned into his scorched flesh.

Clare couldn't speak. She was in shock. There was gasp of horror from the group watching from the base of the helipad. They knew what their fate would be now.

Matt was trying to hold back tears of frustration and helplessness. He'd really thought that Clare might make it out alive, perhaps even manage to rescue them. She looked crushed as Yanis marched her over to join the rest of the group. Vinden and Gina were sobbing now. Those who were in couples were holding each other. Kylie looked furious. Like Matt she was desperate to fight back.

As Clare neared the main group, there was the distinctive sound of helicopter blades once again. They all looked up to the idling helicopter on the pad to their side, but the noise wasn't coming from there. A flashlight appeared out of the gloom, swooping across the main deck and making a fast pass over the fort.

'They're onto us!' shouted Baptiste. 'Come on, we need to clear out. Get the copter ready, Yanis. We're leaving!'

For the first time since he'd met her, Matt saw that Victoria looked unnerved. This had taken them by surprise. They'd thought they had the run of the fort.

The second helicopter had circled around and was now making another sweep of the deck. The searchlight illuminated the small group. Somebody had come to help them. But with the helipad occupied, there didn't seem much that they could do.

'Yanis, radio the hangar to tell him we're on our way. The boats will take at least another twenty minutes to get here. We're still good to go. Victoria, get Helix! The rest of you, lie face down on the deck.'

This was it. Matt knew how this was ending. Baptiste would climb up on the helipad, shoot them and then fly off. Clare moved over to him, squeezed his hand and stroked his arm. It could be the last time they ever touched.

'I'm so sorry I dragged you into all this, Clare. I should have been happy with what we had.'

'It's okay, Matt. I'm sorry I gave you a tough time over those photos. I just thought ... Well, you know what I thought. It doesn't matter. I love you. And at least we're together now.'

Matt and Clare joined the others, face down, hands placed at the back of their heads. Yanis had fired up the helicopter and the blades were beginning to pick up speed. The second chopper was buzzing them overhead. Another few minutes and it would all be over. There was nothing more they could do.

CHAPTER THIRTY

October, Helix Fort

As Baptiste stepped towards the ladder to climb up to the helipad, Gina sat up and began pleading for their lives.

'Take everything we have! Just let everybody live. We don't know anything about you. You can escape from here. Please, no more deaths.'

Baptiste turned around and struck her head with the butt of his machine gun. She collapsed on the ground, a deep gash in her forehead. As David was moving to help her, out of nowhere came the growl of two dogs. With his back now turned, and his first foot on the ladder, the dogs began to snap at the ankles of the man who'd hurt their beloved mistress.

Where the animals had been all that time was anybody's guess. Perhaps they had been cowering after their earlier altercation with the first gunman. They seemed to smell the danger and were doing their best to slow down Baptiste, but they were no match for a man of his size and physique. Once he'd realised what was happening, he kicked them away.

But it was all that Matt, Clare and Kylie needed – the tiniest of windows in which to turn things around.

'Take cover!' Matt screamed.

Gina, David, Vinden and Phyllis were old and slow, and had barely registered what was going on by the time the younger group were on their feet. Eddy was still struggling too. He just wasn't fast enough.

Baptiste spun around, his gun trained on Quentin and Hunter, who were running towards the hot tubs, the closest cover that was available to them. There was a series of sharp cracks and Quentin dropped to the floor. Hunter skidded in behind the tub as a bullet struck the panel to the side of him. Alby was running across the deck in pursuit. Caught in the crossfire, he crashed to the ground, dead.

Matt, Kylie and Clare were running to the bar area only to come face to face with Victoria. In front of her was Sebastian, his hands and mouth no longer taped up. She levelled her pistol and fired two shots at Kylie, striking her in the shoulder once. She dropped to the floor. Matt and Clare froze.

'Walk them over. And bring the bitch as security!' Baptiste shouted, pointing at Clare.

'Over there!' Victoria instructed. Kylie was whimpering in pain on the floor in front of her. Matt moved back, separated from his wife once again.

'Further back!' she shouted, levelling her gun.

'No!' cried Clare. 'Please no!'

As Victoria squeezed the trigger, Kylie spotted a last opportunity to help before she passed out completely. Taking a leaf out of the dogs' book, she bit hard into Victoria's ankle. The bullet went wide, missing Matt completely.

Victoria shook her off and pointed her gun towards Sebastian and Clare, indicating that they should head for the helicopter.

Baptiste had given up the idea of shooting everybody now. He was more preoccupied with the helicopter, which was continuing to buzz the deck. All he wanted was to be off the fort. Victoria was right behind him, rushing over to the helicopter with her hostages. They climbed up the ladder to the helipad. Matt was following them, waving the older group out of harm's way as he crossed the deck to the ladder.

Ahead of him he could see Baptiste climbing into the chopper. He reached the top of the ladder and ran towards Clare. Yanis had the machine hovering just above the platform, ready to take off at any moment. Baptiste was on the other side of the cabin, taking aim at the second helicopter, which was getting close to the fort. He took a few shots and missed.

Matt knew that Victoria was out of bullets. With Baptiste preoccupied, if he timed it right, he could grab Clare and pull her to safety. If he could help Sebastian too, he would, but Clare was his priority. The thugs wouldn't hurt Sebastian Helix. He was an asset and presumably they were going to earn a hefty ransom from him.

Clare stepped up onto the helicopter, followed directly by Victoria.

'Clare, jump!' Matt shouted, running towards her. The helicopter lifted a little higher away from the pad as Yanis prepared to take off. Matt leapt towards his wife, and as he did so, she extended her hand to meet his. He had her in his grip.

'Jump, I've got you!' he called. Victoria pointed the gun at him and pulled the trigger. Nothing. Matt had been counting the bullets. He knew he was safe. As Clare moved to jump, Baptiste swung across the cabin and grabbed her by the collar of her boiler suit. She hung there for a moment as the helicopter began to lift. Baptiste pulled her back into the cabin and her hand slipped out of Matt's.

'No!' he called, as the chopper reached his shoulder height. Then 'Fuck it!' as he clasped the machine's landing skid and held on for dear life.

The helicopter rose from the helipad, and then suddenly veered off into the darkness with Matt swinging beneath, desperately holding onto the metal rail. He could hear Clare screaming in the cabin above his head. She thought he'd fallen, but Victoria had seen what he'd done. All Baptiste's attention was on the second helicopter, which was now flying dangerously close to them. He was getting increasingly frustrated at his inability to get a direct shot at his opponent.

Matt caught a glimpse of the pilot. It was Tucker Gee. He'd come to help them. He was trying to drive Yanis back towards the fort.

Matt's arms were burning. The jolting movements and constant changes of direction tore at his sinews. He couldn't stay there much longer. He was stuck, he simply didn't have the strength to pull himself up to the cabin.

There was the sound of machine-gun fire as Baptiste used the last of the bullets in his magazine.

'Shit!'

Baptiste's cursing could be heard over the sound of the blades. Tucker had become emboldened now. He was blocking their path and forcing the chopper back towards the fort.

Matt considered dropping down into the sea below him. He could see that Tucker was trying to force them to land,

and they were descending towards the deck now. In the distance were three boats. One was orange. It was the lifeguard – he was as certain as he could be of that. If he and Clare jumped into the water, they'd be located quickly. They could survive that.

The helicopter was steadier now, hovering at a height of about a hundred metres above the deck. For the first time, Matt noticed a step positioned below the cabin door. If he could haul himself up to that, perhaps he would be able to drag himself up into the cabin after all.

Tucker saw what he was trying to do and pulled over to the opposite side, above the other helicopter, forcing it into a tight circle above the fort. Matt summoned all his strength and managed to heave himself up onto the step. Clare had seen him. She was hanging onto a handrail, terrified. The doors were wide open and the wind was cutting through the cabin.

Matt could see inside now. Baptiste, Victoria and Sebastian were all shouting instructions to Yanis, watching Tucker's dangerous manoeuvres to their side. It didn't make sense. What was Sebastian Helix doing? It didn't feel right.

Clare reached out to pull Matt into the cabin. He moved his hand onto the railing as the helicopter swung violently around again, dodging Tucker. Matt realised there were two of them – a second helicopter was working with Tucker to force Yanis into landing.

Baptiste, sensing that something had changed in the cabin, turned around to see Matt behind him. Matt ran towards him, caught him off guard and pushed him out of the open door. As the helicopter spun around, he hit the tail blade and the chopper started to spiral out of control.

'Jump, Clare! Jump out!' Matt shouted.

Victoria looked around for a weapon. Both guns were

now useless. As the helicopter began to spin then fall, the accomplices glanced at each other. For a moment it looked as if they were going to try to fight him. Sebastian found a small fire extinguisher to his side. He reached for it, pulled it from the retaining clip and waved it towards Matt. Was he in on this? How could he possibly be involved? It was ridiculous.

'Damn it, Sebastian. It's over,' Matt said. 'Whatever is going on, you should land the helicopter and walk away from it all.'

'We can't, Seb,' Victoria cried. 'The only way we can make it out of this is if Matt and Clare die. Then we can walk away. We can make it look however we want to.'

Matt could hear a police loudhailer warning the pilot to come down to land. The helicopters were flying perilously close to each other. The boats were almost at the landing platform now.

Matt looked towards his wife.

'Trust me, Clare. Jump!' he shouted.

Her face white with terror, Clare closed her eyes and leapt out of the helicopter.

As she disappeared into the night, Sebastian Helix swung the fire extinguisher at Matt's head. He dropped to the floor of the cabin, dazed, his face covered in blood. Sebastian struck him again. This time he didn't get up. The last thing he heard was a command from the police helicopter, the message drowned out by the persistent sound of the rotors. The helicopter began to spin again, dropping like a bag of bricks out of the sky.

It crashed into the side of the fort, crushing the cabin, dropped down into the wild sea and exploded.

EPILOGUE

November, Helix Fort

'You certainly rushed that out!' Clare laughed, squeezing Kylie's hand. It was good to be relaxing together again. For the past few weeks life had been an endless round of hospital visits, police calls and legal consultations.

'You don't sit on a news story like that. I know it was a terrible thing to happen, but for a writer this is gold dust.'

Clare had run up from the boat to see her friend. They'd formed an instant bond on Helix Fort and it was a friendship neither wanted to let slip. She'd decided to forego the option of a helicopter ride. She was done with helicopters. It would take her some time before she could even face an aeroplane.

They were at No Man's Fort, one of the other converted forts situated just off Portsmouth in the Solent. This one was a four-star luxury hotel with over twenty bedrooms. If you peered out to sea, you'd catch a glimpse of Helix Fort, which was currently up for sale. It would no doubt be purchased by some other millionaire, maybe even a hotel chain keen to cash in on its new notoriety.

It was Kylie's book launch and the entire fort was packed with press, celebrities and friends. It was the perfect location for the event. Clare wondered for a moment how delightful their meal with Sebastian might have been if their weekend at Helix Fort had gone to plan.

There was the sound of barking. Clare knew immediately who it was. Gina came into the room, still with the remains of a scab on her forehead. David was with her holding Scooby tightly in his arms. Clare fussed over the little dog.

'How is he now?' she asked, stooping down to stroke the other two animals. She'd taken a liking to them. They'd all got to know each other a little better on that lifeboat ride back to Portsmouth. They'd all shared something terrible, they were bonded for life now.

'If it wasn't for Matt, this poor little fellow would definitely have died,' said Gina. 'We're so grateful for what he did. He was in such danger too. It was so thoughtful.'

There was a moment of silence as they each considered what Matt had sacrificed for them that night. He was the one person who should have been in that lifeboat with them. As they sat there, relieved that it was over, they all knew how much they owed him.

'Oh, there's Jerry. I didn't think he'd make it. Excuse me, everyone. I must go to speak to him.'

Clare patted Scooby one more time and headed over to Jerry. His hand was so heavily bandaged, it looked like he was wearing a plaster cast. He was drinking an orange juice.

Cautiously Clare moved in to hug him.

'It's so good to see you, Jerry. I can't believe they saved your finger.'

'I have you and Kylie to thank for that. If you hadn't put it in the freezer, who knows what might have happened.'

'I saw the story of the operation in the Sunday papers. It's amazing what they can do.'

'Yeah, it looked disgusting, but it saved the finger. Replantation is the process they used. The surgeon reckons I might even get some small movement in it. No more guitar for me though. That's finished.'

'I see the back catalogue is topping the charts again. That must be a big help.'

'Yes, it helps with the money. But I'm back with my wife and kids again, and that's all I care about. I need to forget this rock star nonsense and become plain old Jerry Daniels.'

He nodded and smiled at a beautiful woman in an elegant blue silk dress sitting at one of the far tables. She looked relaxed and as she moved her head, her glossy black hair brushed her shoulders. She waved back and two young children came running over to him, burrowing into his legs.

'Look at these two beauties,' Jerry beamed. 'Three beauties,' he added as his wife joined them. 'What could ever be more important than this?'

Clare was missing Matt. Suddenly the room felt desperately empty without him. She felt guilty.

There was an excited flurry of chatter, then a round of applause. He'd arrived. She'd been in such a rush to see Kylie that she let him hobble up the staircase with Vinden and Phyllis. She reckoned that was about the right speed while he was still using crutches. Quentin and Hunter were following behind with Eddy. Quentin was wired up in a neck brace and his right arm was in plaster. Eddy looked slightly better off, but his older skin was struggling to rid itself of the bruises it had sustained.

'We look like we should be in a hospital waiting room, not a posh book launch!' Matt laughed.

'How's your leg?' Jerry asked, squeezing Matt's arm with his good hand.

'Ouch, careful Jerry. That's sore too! Getting better thanks. I'll always have a slight limp according to my physio, but it could have been a lot worse. I'm so pleased you kept your finger.'

Matt choked up, his eyes filling with tears. They'd seen and done terrible things that night. But most of them had got out of there. Clare and Matt, with help from the others, had saved lives. And now they were there to celebrate the launch of Kylie's new book: *Sebastian Helix: Fall of a Millionaire.*

Matt had told Clare he wouldn't be reading it. He said he knew the story well enough already. Clare had got a signed advance copy. She'd gobbled up every word. It was the tale of a marriage gone sour. Sebastian Helix had been sleeping with Victoria Winterton, his PA, as he went through some ridiculous mid-life crisis. It had broken his marriage. Under pressure from a younger woman with elevated expectations, and the weight of a crippling divorce settlement, Sebastian had made a hasty and unwise investment in several fledgeling cryptocurrencies. He hadn't done his due diligence, hoping to make a quick buck, and he'd been badly burned.

The value of his investment collapsed overnight. His finances and company shares were immediately thrown into a nosedive. It was a catastrophe. He was going to lose everything he had built up and his reputation would be destroyed. He was heading for financial ruin. Completely losing his judgment, in desperation he planned an elaborate insurance and kidnapping swindle. And of course it had all gone terribly wrong.

Sebastian Helix and Victoria Winterton had both lost their lives in the crash, while Matt had simply rolled out into the sea as the helicopter spiralled down, unconscious and oblivious. The two of them had been completely delusional. The inquest concluded that even at that stage they still thought they might get away in the helicopter. It was a ridiculous notion, and one which ended in tragedy.

'If you'll excuse me one moment, Jerry, I'll sit down and take the weight off my legs.' Matt said. I'm still struggling with these crutches and those steps up from the boat don't get any easier.'

Kylie walked onto a small stage and welcomed everyone to the book signing. Most people moved to the front to catch a better view of their host. Clare was pleased to be able to hang back and take a seat next to Matt. It looked like he had something to tell her.

'It's confirmed. The email came in while we were in the boat. I read it on the way up the steps. It's over. We won!'

Clare stretched across and hugged him hard.

'It was all legal and the transaction is binding. We've cleared our debts. We're now mortgage-free. With the money to buy the intellectual property rights and an ongoing royalty of 1.5%, that'll set us up for life. And it went through the business, not his personal estate, so they're honouring it.'

'God, I'm so relieved. And to think I thought you'd messed it up by making that deal with Sebastian, Matt. He was a crafty bastard, using Olaf to push your price down and make you believe you might walk away with nothing.'

They held hands across the table, smiling and looking towards Kylie. Matt had shared his fears with Clare that he'd made a terrible misjudgment signing the deal with Sebastian Helix before the meal, but it turned out that it was the millionaire who'd messed things up. For Sebastian Helix, it was to prove a fatal error. For Clare and Matt it had been their one last chance to save themselves from debt, divorce and even death. They'd fought back and made it out alive. They could survive anything now.

If you enjoyed this book, you'll love the Morecambe Bay series of psychological thrillers. Nine books and non-stop suspense. Available in paperback and e-book formats.

NO MORE SECRETS PREVIEW

Spean Bridge, July 1999

Katy watched as the cottage burned. Elijah was in there, unable to escape from the wooden structure as it was engulfed in flames. The fire was ferocious in the wind, with huge flares sweeping across the garden, keeping the huddle of horrified onlookers at bay. The air was filled with the crackle of burning timber and the sobbing of the five friends, distraught at the thought of Elijah trapped inside.

Driven back by the searing heat, they watched in terror, unable to think of any action they could take to extinguish the inferno. They were forced to sit it out and wait until the horror ended. Elijah didn't stand a chance. There was nothing to stop the flames once they'd started, and they consumed the building in less than half an hour.

There were no phone boxes nearby. The cabin was nestled at the foot of a hill, surrounded by trees, and at the end of a long, winding track. Even if help could have been summoned, it would have been too late. They were too far away from the nearest town.

It had seemed like such a good idea: two weeks in the Scottish Highlands, a log cabin in the middle of nowhere, and a car boot filled with booze. They'd finished their year one exams, they had a long summer ahead of them, and they were in love – young, idealistic love, their whole lives yet to live. They had nearly four months away from university and nothing to do with all that time.

Five of them had piled into the car – it was a wonder there was any room for the clothes and toiletries. They didn't care, all they could think of was two weeks of sleeping in, laughter and drinking. But it all took a turn for the worse. The easy-come, easy-go bubble of university life quickly evaporated as the reality of living in a cabin with an erratic boiler and night-time visits from the local vermin set in. The laughter turned to bitching, the booze remained unopened in the fridge, and relationships became tense. What had seemed like too short a time to go on holiday soon turned into an eternity. Two weeks became a lifetime and plans to share a student house in the new term began to look hasty and ill-conceived.

But it never should have come to this. They watched and wept as the wooden structure was transformed into a smoking, charred ruin. Elijah was in there somewhere. There would be nothing left of him, the flames were so fierce. The squabbles seemed so petty now. How had they let it get so out of hand?

Eventually, in the darkness of the night time, the emergency services arrived, alerted by a farmer across the valley. He'd thought it was a woodland fire, started by careless campers. It turned out to be much worse.

When the police got there, they found five shocked friends, standing and watching the scene before them, stunned at what had just happened. It would take them a long time to recover from what they'd seen.

In spite of the tears, Elijah's death was no freak accident, even though it would be sadly recorded as such by the Sheriff. There was a reason why Elijah hadn't escaped to safety, even though he should have got away well before the flames took a grip. Nobody could understand why he hadn't got out, but there was nothing to suggest anything but a tragic sequence of events.

The repercussions of that day would be felt for many years to come. There was always a lingering doubt among the friends, a feeling that somebody could have helped him on that terrible day. Elijah's death could have been avoided. But not everyone had told the truth that night.

No More Secrets is available as a paperback or e-book.

AUTHOR NOTES

One Last Chance was written very much in the same vein as Dead of Night in that it is a non-stop, fast-paced and action-driven psychological thriller.

The action begins in the first chapter with one of the main characters losing his finger.

I hope that didn't put you off your tea!

I think it was the setting of this book that got me most excited.

I wanted to place my characters in a location where they could be isolated and exposed.

I used this technique in my psychological thriller called So Many Lies.

It's a bit like Agatha Christie's *And Then There Were None* in that I wanted to force a group of different characters in a location where they were stuck with each other and had to see whatever horrible things happening to them through to the bitter end, until help arrived.

The main action of this story is set on a fictional version of the Solway Forts which are located in the Solent off the UK mainland.

These forts are amazing!

There are three of them and two forts can be visited by the public.

You can even host celebrations there, stay overnight or go for afternoon tea.

The forts are reached by boat and to access the structures you have to clamber up steps which run along the outside of the imposing, circular structures.

Because so many nasty things happen in my book, I decided that I had better set the action on a fictional version of the forts - I didn't want to wreck the tourist industry!

My imaginary fort has been taken over by Sebastian Helix who has spared no expense on refurbishing the dilapidated building and turned it into a millionaire's paradise.

I referenced the real-life Solent Forts when I was writing my story and all of the elements that are mentioned in One Last Chance are authentic and realistic.

I haven't actually visited the forts yet, but I do intend to do that at a later date.

I'm very fortunate that so many photographs are available showing every element of those amazing structures to enable me to plot out my story.

I really enjoyed creating the characters of Matt and Clare and as with all of my psychological thrillers this poor old couple are thrust into financial difficulties and precarious circumstances from the get-go.

I have a phrase on my pin board in my office which says 'scary things happen to ordinary people' and I wrote that down after interviewing psychological thriller writer Mark Edwards on my writing podcast.

It struck me that is exactly what I need to be portraying in my stories and so in every plot that I devise I try to come up with as many terrible things that can happen to ordinary people as possible.

Thanks for the tip Mark!

Clare's experiences working in a restaurant based on my own teenage years.

From the age of 13 until the age of 18 I worked as a waiter in the village restaurant alongside many of my teenage friends who also lived locally.

It was a great place to work and I thoroughly enjoyed my work in catering.

We had a lot of fun with the customers as well as having a great time as a staff.

Later on, whilst at college, I went on to work as a waiter at a holiday camp for a summer season.

(That experience was the inspiration for Left for Dead!)

I can remember earning an excellent tip from a group of women who were eating at the restaurant one night.

As you would expect, they were little bit tipsy towards the end of their meal and one of the selections on the sweet menu looked, let's say, a little suggestive when I placed them on the tables in front of them.

The ladies were laughing their heads off and I, of course, played up to it!

That earned me a big tip and I based Clare's experiences in the restaurant - when she unbuttoned her blouse a little on the advice of Zoe - on my real-life experience waiting on tables.

Matt's dilemma is very much based on own journey as an entrepreneur.

I worked for the BBC for 18 years then decided to take voluntary redundancy and strike out on my own.

It's that journey that has led to me writing and publishing books like this one.

I have absolutely loved every minute of being self-employed and making my own way in the world, but I won't pretend that it's always easy and it can be very frightening when you leave the security of a salary for the first time.

When I left the BBC I had a growing family of three children and so felt the same pressure that Matt does to bring the money in and keep a roof over his head.

So although the plot line involving Matt is not my own story, it is very much based on my thoughts and observations.

Incidentally, I was also involved in a tech competition like Matt - which I won-to create an app for mobile devices - so I know that process well, even though my prize was nowhere near as big as his.

One of the problems I experience as a UK writer is not being able to give characters access to guns and other powerful weaponry.

I like to keep my books authentic and in the UK I would not be able to get my hands on a gun without some difficulty, as a regular member of the public.

Because we're dealing with mercenaries in One Last Chance it was easier for me to incorporate weaponry in this book, but Matt - of course - has no experience in this area so he's very much out of his depth.

As with all of my books my heroes are regular people - they have no special skills, they have very little experience of violence and the situations in which they find themselves are unimaginable in their daily lives.

You may have been amused by the use of dogs in this book and as a lover of the animals I was keen to include a couple of scenes which involve them.

If you've ever watched *House of Cards* on Netflix you may

remember that Kevin Spacey kills a wounded dog in the first episode and there's a thought in writing circles that you can show a lot about a character by the way they treat animals.

So Matt rescues one of the dogs and in doing so shows that he has a good heart.

The character of Olaf was based very much on my feelings as a weakling at secondary school who was no good at sport.

Matt is physically intimidated by Olaf who seems to have it all - the great body, sporting prowess and supreme self-confidence.

He gets his comeuppance and shows his true colours and Clare's good sense prevails in her choice of Matt as her companion.

Matt is a good guy, even though for much of the book you may suspect that he has betrayed Claire, there are plenty of hints along the way that he can be trusted and isn't a rat, like Olaf.

When it came to the rich characters I didn't want them to be silly or caricatured, but I needed a cast of people whose wealth would intimidate Matt and Claire.

When I was creating the character of Jerry I always had Slash in my mind, although he is not particularly based upon that real-life guitarist.

I had a lot of fun with Vinden and Phyllis who are based on a rather quaint couple I met at a UK property event that I attended.

Kylie is another journalist drawn out of my own experience of working 18 years in the BBC and she's a tough cookie, even though it's not always clear that her motives are pure.

As for David and Gina I must admit to including them

for comedy value, hence the dogs and the various scenes which involve them.

We have a wide array of characters in this story and I thoroughly enjoyed isolating them on the fort, creating a horrific situation and letting it all play out.

We even get to play with some big toys in this story, like helicopters and boats, which is always fun.

I hope you enjoyed reading One Last Chance and that it will inspire you to check out more of my thrillers.

If you liked this story and want to stay in touch, I'd be delighted if you registered for my email updates at https://paulteague.net/thrillers, as that's where I share news of what I'm writing and tell you about any reader discounts and freebies that are available.

Paul Teague

ALSO BY PAUL J. TEAGUE

Morecambe Bay Trilogy 1

Book 1 - Left For Dead

Book 2 - Circle of Lies

Book 3 - Truth Be Told

Morecambe Bay Trilogy 2

Book 4 - Trust Me Once

Book 5 - Fall From Grace

Book 6 - Bound By Blood

Morecambe Bay Trilogy 3

Book 7 - First To Die

Book 8 - Nothing To Lose

Book 9 - Last To Tell

Note: The Morecambe Bay trilogies are best read in the order shown above.

Don't Tell Meg Trilogy

Features DCI Kate Summers and Steven Terry.

Book 1 - Don't Tell Meg

Book 2 - The Murder Place

Book 3 - The Forgotten Children

Standalone Thrillers

Dead of Night

No More Secrets

So Many Lies

Two Years After

Friends Who Lie

Now You See Her

ABOUT THE AUTHOR

Hi, I'm Paul Teague, the author of the Morecambe Bay series and the Don't Tell Meg trilogy, as well as several other standalone psychological thrillers such as One Last Chance, Dead of Night and No More Secrets.

I'm a former broadcaster and journalist with the BBC, but I have also worked as a primary school teacher, a disc jockey, a shopkeeper, a waiter and a sales rep.

I've read thrillers all my life, starting with Enid Blyton's Famous Five series as a child, then graduating to James Hadley Chase, Harlan Coben, Linwood Barclay and Mark Edwards.

Let's get connected!
https://paulteague.net